PENGUIN BOOKS
UNDER THE BAKUL TREE

Dr Mrinal Kalita received the Sahitya Akademi's Bal Sahitya Puraskar 2021 for his seminal debut, *Bakul Phular Dare*, which became an overnight bestseller. The book has gone on to redefine the coming-of-age novel in Assamese and is now in its forty-second edition. The novel was narrated in thirty-two episodes on the novel reading programme of All India Radio, Guwahati, in 2020 and has been made into a feature film.

A professor of mathematics by profession, Kalita's short stories have been translated into English, Hindi, Odia and Bengali. 'Jooj', one of Kalita's stories for young adults, has been included in the syllabus of CBSE and SEBA. The story 'Ajantrik' (Not a Machine) was published in *adda*—the prestigious online literary magazine of the Commonwealth Foundation.

Kalita's short-story collections include *Anuxilon* (Practice), *Ajantrik Anuxilon* (Non-mechanical Practice) and *Mrityur Xipare* (Beyond Death). His non-fiction oeuvre features *Godfatheror Haat Aru Satanor Mogoju* (Godfather's Hands and Satan's Brain), *Gonitor Bornil Jogot* (The Colourful World of Mathematics) and *Okopote: Mor Aru Prithivir* (Candidly Me: The World and I).

Partha Pratim Goswami has translated several notable Assamese works, such as Mamoni Raisom Goswami's *Sanskara* and Mrinal Kalita's *Ketela Pohur Kait*. Goswami is intrigued by the exacting process of reimagining a writer's world while trying to convey the cadences and nuances of the regional language into English. Goswami's areas of interest include comparative literature, Indian writing in English and translation studies. He is the chief translator of the Translation Wing at Gauhati High Court, Assam. Goswami's wish is to make influential literary works in Assamese available to global readers.

UNDER THE BAKUL TREE

MRINAL KALITA

Translated from the Assamese by
PARTHA PRATIM GOSWAMI

PENGUIN BOOKS

An imprint of Penguin Random House

PENGUIN BOOKS

USA | Canada | UK | Ireland | Australia
New Zealand | India | South Africa | China | Singapore

Penguin Books is part of the Penguin Random House group of companies
whose addresses can be found at global.penguinrandomhouse.com

Published by Penguin Random House India Pvt. Ltd
4th Floor, Capital Tower 1, MG Road,
Gurugram 122 002, Haryana, India

First published in Penguin Books by Penguin Random House India 2024

Text copyright © Mrinal Chandra Kalita 2024
Translation copyright © Partha Pratim Goswami 2024

ISBN 9780143458579

Typeset in Bembo Std by Manipal Technologies Limited, Manipal

www.penguin.co.in

Dear Ribrib!

This is the long story your Bapa has been writing all this while. You told me when I finished writing this book, you would go up to people, raise the book high with both hands and proudly say, 'This is a book written by my Bapa!'

This is that book.

So Ribrib, your Bapa's book is now yours!

Your Bapa
12 September 2023

1

A melancholic feeling seemed to have gripped Ashim's mind. Sitting alone under the bakul tree beyond the school gate, he stared listlessly as his schoolmates passed him without sparing a glance. None among them cared to call out to him. He too didn't feel the urge to wave at any of them. These days, Ashim preferred to keep to himself. He felt uncomfortable when someone approached him or talked to him. He felt he was a millipede that would coil into itself, like a roll, if touched.

The results of their annual examinations had been declared earlier that day, but Ashim didn't feel like checking them. He was not sure whether he had passed or failed. He had no reason to rejoice even if he did manage to pass, nor had anything to lament about if he had failed. Last year, Ashim had somehow managed to scrape through, but there had been a downward spiral in his performance at school. Truth be told, over the past couple of years, he had lost the urge to study. All he did now was ponder about different things, sitting beneath the blossoming bakul tree.

Gradually, the hordes of school kids walking past him reduced to a trickle. They left for their homes in groups, chattering noisily.

The day was drawing to a close, and the school campus was almost deserted. Ashim was now quite bored and weary. He got up sluggishly and thought of taking a quick look at his results. He walked into the premises and started making his way towards the noticeboard where the results were pinned up. Suddenly, a sense of fear overtook him. The noticeboard was in front of the office room, and Ashim was sure he would be scolded if he crossed paths with any of his teachers. His palpitation increased. He staggered as he moved closer to the noticeboard. His throat started drying up. Somehow, he gathered his inner strength and reached the board. His eyes scanned for the result sheet of class IX. *Ah!* Nirmal had retained his first rank this time too. He felt a stab of pain in his chest. *Uff,* he thought, searching for his name. He had passed! He had actually managed to pass! Though his name appeared at the bottom of the list, he too had been somehow promoted to class X. Just as he was processing this information, something else took over his mind, disturbing him. An unfinished chain of thoughts came back and started niggling at him again. Ashim decided it was time to go home.

Suddenly, a shrill voice rang through the air.

'Come here, you idiot!'

Ashim was startled! He turned around to see that it was none other than Mahendra sir! *Perhaps, he too is about to leave for home*, hoped Ashim. A young man accompanied his teacher. Ashim didn't know him, but he was oddly frightened and embarrassed at the same time. Mahendra sir was a strict disciplinarian, and Ashim knew that sir was on the verge of scolding him. Ashim had no objection to getting reprimanded by his teachers as he was used to it by now. But he was not prepared to get admonished in front of a complete stranger. Perhaps he would have to get used to this too over the course of time; who knew?

The boy gingerly went up to the teacher and stood in front of him, with his head bowed and hands pressed tightly against his body.

All of a sudden, a hard slap landed on Ashim's cheek.

'You're ruined,' roared Mahendra sir. He then turned to the person at his side and said, 'Once, this boy was the topper of his class.'

Thick tears rolled down Ashim's cheek, and a second later, they dropped to the ground. But Mahendra sir ignored them and rushed towards the gate, angrily shaking the corner of his dhoti which he had been holding in his hand.

But the young, unfamiliar, unknown man didn't budge.

Standing in front of a perfect stranger, Ashim felt quite awkward. His mind was filled with shame and embarrassment. When his teacher had called out to him, he knew a rebuke was coming, but he didn't expect to be slapped, that too in front of a stranger. He turned around to leave.

The young man called out to him, 'What's your name?'

'A–Ashim,' mumbled the boy in a hoarse voice. He was filled with sorrow and humiliation.

'That's a nice name you've got!'

Saying this, the man left hurriedly for the gate. Mahendra master was waiting for him outside.

Ashim stared in the direction of the young man's departure. He found it strange that the person didn't try to ridicule him.

However, very soon, Ashim's thoughts returned to what he had been thinking about when he had been sitting under the tree. A feeling of intense sadness enveloped him again. As he put one foot in front of the other, he turned around to take a good look at the school building.

Just then, he saw Nirmal running towards him. Nirmal was the boy who had been securing the first rank for the past two years. Before that, Ashim was the one who used to top the class. Nirmal always came second. It was all before Ashim's performance started deteriorating.

Ashim felt quite embarrassed upon seeing Nirmal. After all, the boy had replaced him on the academic throne. *Nirmal is a good, sharp student. And me . . . I . . . I am a bad student and getting worse by the day.*

Ashim grew restless. A strange sort of despair mixed with a twinge of jealousy made him feel weak and fidgety. Anger, too, began to stir inside him. But Ashim had no idea what the source of his anger was. He felt an intense urge to run away from everything. He left for the gate hurriedly, pretending as if he had not seen Nirmal approach him.

'A-shi-m!' Nirmal's shout echoed in the huge, silent school campus before dying down in Ashim's heart.

Ashim halted just outside the gate as Nirmal reached him.

'You are yet to leave for home, Nirmal?' Ashim tried to smile at Nirmal with a congratulatory look.

Nirmal stared at his classmate. He found it hard to tell Ashim that, in fact, he had been waiting for an opportunity to find him alone. But not knowing how to initiate the conversation, Nirmal remained silent.

Ashim felt uneasy now. In order to break the ice, Ashim tried again. 'You've done well in the exam!' he said a little too loudly, trying to summon a natural-looking smile.

But Nirmal was not elated at Ashim's words. He replied softly, 'I don't feel good about securing the first position, you know.'

After a pause, Nirmal spoke again—

'The position was not meant for *me*, Ashim.'

An awkward silence hung over them.

Ashim was speechless. The flame of jealousy which had been flickering inside him extinguished in the blink of an eye. He wondered how this 'unfamiliar Nirmal' had been hiding underneath the all too familiar one, the boy that everyone knew! *How pure at heart could he be? He appears unhappy despite securing the first rank!* thought Ashim, feeling small in front of this sensitive boy. His eyes became moist, and he started to feel very uneasy.

Neither of them uttered a word after that awkward exchange.

Gradually, darkness descended around the bakul tree near the school gate. A gust of cold wind started blowing in from the riverside and in that cool darkness, Nirmal's gently spoken words mingled with the breeze. 'Ashim, will you tell me what is bothering you?'

Ashim felt as if his heart would burst. He was choking with emotions. He felt like crying aloud.

Abruptly, Ashim turned and started running away. He needed to escape from Nirmal. He ran and ran, disappearing ultimately at the turn of the road.

2

Ashim lay sleepless on the bed. He was restless. The moonlight crept in through the slats in the reed-mat wall and scattered on the opposite side. He could see the starry sky through the slats. Ashim didn't like it in the slightest. He didn't like the scattered moonlight floating inside the house and he found no beauty in the star-filled sky that appeared to him through the slats in the wall. The scattered moonlight looked like lumps on the skin of a leper! As the thought crossed his mind, he felt a sudden jolt in his body. He felt as if he was becoming mentally ill.

For the last few days, he had been thinking about the same thing over and over again. But he couldn't arrive at a decision. He turned to look at the face of his Deuta, his father, who was fast asleep beside him on the same cot. He then looked at his mother and sister who were sleeping on the next cot. He could see their pale, run-down faces in the moonlight. An acute pang of pain filled his heart. His feelings towards his mother and sister were always very clear. However, that was not the case with his father. He was never quite at ease around him. And, of course, he didn't know whether to feel sorry for his father or be angry at him. Whenever he had to face him, a kind of uneasiness weighed Ashim down.

Ashim got out of his bed silently. Removing the horizontal bamboo pole which held the door shut, he opened the door and stepped out of the house. Cowbells rang a couple of times in the cowshed. Occasionally, hoots of owls came travelling from somewhere. Dew drops were dripping relentlessly and a thick veil of mist shrouded the area. Shivering in the cold, Ashim got down from the veranda and went to the cowshed to fetch a bundle of firewood which his mother kept there as cooking fuel. Then, taking out the small kerosene lamp from the house, he tried to light a fire. It was only after a few tries that the fire began to burn properly.

As the warmth from the burning logs soothed him, Ashim tried to analyse the whole matter with a calm mind. He would need a sizeable amount of money for admission into class X as well as for buying textbooks, notebooks and so on. Moreover, after a few months, he would again need money to fill up the form for the matriculation examination. And even if he was able to pass his board exams, he couldn't dream of studying in a college. His sister, Ajoli, had been promoted to class VII this year. Up to class VIII, the government provided all the textbooks and exempted school fees for female students, but after two years, money would be needed for her studies too and he needed to think about that. On the other hand, his father's income by now had dwindled to almost nothing. Occasionally, his father earned a little bit of money by working as a daily wager. But whatever little his father earned, was always used up by himself.

Ashim turned his thoughts away from his father for the time being, as it would only demoralize him further. He thought of his mother. He felt deeply for her. It concerned him that her health was deteriorating day by day. Apart from doing all the household chores, she worked as a house help for two or three families. In return, she received some rice and vegetables. On top of all this work, she also had to look after the cow.

And what do I do? I only study.

Ashim felt that he was a burden on his mother's shoulders. As he thought about it all, over and over, staring into the fire, his head became heavy. Then, all of a sudden, not wanting to dwell on his thoughts any further, Ashim made a firm resolve. It was done.

He had decided. He would no longer attend school. As it is, his academic performance had deteriorated to the point where he could not even dream of passing the matriculation examination. If he gave up going to school, Ashim decided that he would get enough time to provide some respite to his mother. As he thought about it, he felt a bit lighter. All these days, thinking about the same thing in a relentless loop had drained him both physically and mentally. But now, after taking this decision, he felt much lighter, as if an unbearable burden had been lifted off his head.

All he had to do now was convey his decision to his family. He knew his father wouldn't have any problem, as the man didn't even know which class his son was in. But yes, his mother would be opposed to this idea. She would be deeply hurt, and then she would weep. But Ashim also knew that this sort of lamentation would continue only for a few days. And of course, he would try to convince her if the current state of affairs continued, she would have to cry every day to run the house. Leaving school would be a reason for just a few days' mourning in comparison. Yes, he would persuade her.

Ashim began to feel the chill in the air again. He glanced at the fire—it had already burnt out.

Ah! Although he had been staring at the fire, he hadn't noticed when it had died out. The pit was giving off copious amounts of smoke, which now blew towards his face, making his eyes sting. Ashim stood up.

'Ashim, will you tell me what is bothering you?'

Ashim was taken aback. He turned and saw his mother standing on the threshold with her eyes fixed on him.

Nirmal too had asked him the same question the previous day.

But he couldn't tell anyone what had happened to him. No, he couldn't share this with anyone at all!

3

Ashim had not attended school for a week now. This made Nirmal uneasy. The boy had been noticing astonishing changes in Ashim over the last two years, especially since Ashim had started brooding, sitting under the bakul tree when all his other classmates were busy playing or engaged in other activities that adolescents enjoyed. *Only god knew what he kept thinking about,* he mused. When they had first taken admission in class V at the current school, after primary school was over, Ashim had been the brightest student in their class. He'd come first for three consecutive years. Nirmal was always second until they reached class VIII. That year, Ashim had slipped to the fifteenth position from the first rank in the annual examinations. And now, in the annual examination of class IX, he had moved down further to the forty-seventh position—the last boy in the class. This was why Mahendra master had slapped Ashim in a fit of anger on the day of the results. Nirmal had witnessed the incident from a distance, but he didn't let Ashim know about it.

That day, Nirmal had wanted to meet Ashim all alone. So he'd waited till all his schoolmates had left for home. And then the incident took place. Would anyone who saw it believe that there was a time when Ashim had been Mahendra master's favourite student? But that slap hurt Nirmal too because, now, Nirmal was elevated to the position of their teacher's favourite student. But Nirmal felt as if he had unfairly snatched away the teacher's affection from his former favourite student, Ashim.

Nirmal also knew that Ashim was intelligent enough to not be bothered by all this and that there must be a bigger, more serious problem that he was facing. Nirmal suspected this was such a problem that it did not allow Ashim to study properly, or to play with his friends, or to even laugh to one's heart's content when the teacher was saying something really funny.

Nirmal decided he must find out what had happened to Ashim. It was also bothering him that Ashim had run away from him the other day. He had simply fled. And now, Ashim had not been to school for the last six days. *He can't be allowed to run away like this*, thought Nirmal. No! He would go to Ashim's house that very evening. He had to find out what had happened to his classmate that had transformed him so drastically.

4

From Monday to Saturday, six days had elapsed, but Ashim didn't go to school. When the boy had told his mother about dropping out of school, she was dumbfounded. She had howled and cried. She tried her best to persuade him to rethink this stupid decision. She even suggested that if he had found it difficult to afford textbooks and other stationery items the previous year, she could work in a couple of more households to bump up their earnings. But Ashim wasn't in the mood to hear all this. His reply was short and clear—he wouldn't study any further.

His mother then blamed her husband and held him responsible for Ashim's unthinkable decision. She rebuked her husband for what was happening in their house and the role he had played in their son's downfall. But his father merely replied, 'If he doesn't wish to study further, so be it. What will he become by studying more anyway? An officer?'

Ashim didn't utter anything and silently witnessed this parental conflict. As a matter of course, Ashim's student life died a premature death without creating any ripple anywhere.

Ashim now had plenty of time on his hands. He had already planned what he would do after dropping out of school. For the last six days, he had been working as a labourer, splitting stones in the quarry of his fellow villager, Dibakar dada. He earned Rs 20 if he broke down enough stones to fill a large mustard-oil tin.

Ashim would wake up early nowadays and go to the foothill at eight in the morning. He would take some food with him for lunch, which he would have around midday. After lunch, he would lay out his handwoven gamocha under a tree and rest on it for a bit. He would resume work soon and return home around five in the evening. In a day, he was able to split only three tins' worth of stones, which earned him Rs 60. Every day, upon reaching home, he would give the money to his mother. And each day, his mother told him something sad in a sorrowful tone. Her heart broke seeing the hard toil her son had to undertake every day.

But Ashim felt a sort of contentment.

Of course, it was hard work. After all, it's not at all easy to keep hammering at hard stones for hours. The work needed both strength and patience. At times, Ashim would grunt in fatigue. His shoulders ached as he toiled. He couldn't even sleep well at night as his chest ached due to the physical labour. His face and eyes were coated with fine stone dust. His soft fingers were covered with blisters. The soft skin of his palms had reddened and become rough. The old skin was now starting to peel off. *But no problem*, thought he. In due course of time, it would become easy as he would get used to it. Or so he thought.

Today, Ashim was feeling more tired than usual. He was not well and was feeling dizzy. Because of this, perhaps the hammer had landed on his fingers a couple of times instead of on the stones. One of his fingers had even started to bleed. Perhaps he had tried to break stones a bit faster today, fidgeting due to his ill health. His hands were out of sync, he knew, and that's how the hammer's blow had landed on a finger of his left hand.

Previously, even the sight of blood would scare him, but he was not frightened today. *Breaking the hard rocks has also toughened my mind a bit,* he mused. But his lacerated finger hurt a lot. So, without allowing things to get worse, he returned home early, at four instead of five.

*

Entering the house, he handed over his wages to his mother as usual. Instantly, his mother's eyes fell on the injured finger.

'What has happened to your finger?'

'Nothing,' Ashim said, trying to hide it. But it was not that easy to lie to his mother. The torn piece of cloth wrapped around the finger was glistening with blood.

His mother started sobbing.

'It will heal, Ma,' said Ashim, trying to console her. 'Look, I have applied the juices of *bon xeuli* herb on it, which you had told me have healing properties.'

'Yes, what's the big deal? It will dry up by tomorrow,' rang out his father's unsympathetic voice.

Ashim's heart ached.

His mother gave her husband a stern look.

'Give me the money.' This time his father had spoken, looking at his mother.

His mother kept staring at his father with great anger. But it didn't have any effect. He reiterated, 'I said, give me the money.'

This time, his mother lost her patience. She shuddered with anger and burst out, 'Why do you need money? To drink?'

'That's none of your business!' shouted his father.

His mother shouted with equal intensity, 'Your son has toiled hard to earn this, and you want to squander his hard-earned money on liquor?'

'Oh please. It is the duty of children to look after their parents,' replied his father blandly.

'What? He dropped out of school because of your bad habits. Now he has to give you money for your liquor too?' His mother looked at her husband incredulously.

'Of course!'

'Don't you have any shame?'

Before Ashim could comprehend anything, he found his mother flat on the floor. His father had slapped her with an inordinate amount of force. Then, just as a carnivore snatches a fresh piece of meat, his father snatched the money from his mother's hand. Dumbfounded, Ashim stood shell-shocked.

Anger, sorrow, shame and embarrassment, all had made Ashim's mother extremely restless. Still lying on the floor, she cried mournfully. Meanwhile, hearing the fracas between her parents, Ashim's sister Ajoli came running. Seeing her mother in that state, she also started crying. Meanwhile, his father started hurling filthy abuses at his wife and Ashim.

But this was not the first time that his father had been abusive. For Ashim, this incident was all too familiar. Every evening, the same occurrence took place. Bullying his mother and, if he felt like it, beating her up, his father would snatch whatever his mother could manage to earn. He would go out and use that money to drink and upon returning home, would turn abusive. He would fling Ashim's books around and rough up his wife. After that, he would get tired, lie down on his cot and sleep like a log.

Whenever such a situation arose, Ashim would be at a loss for what to do next. Fright and stress took his breath away. He could hear his heart pumping. He would first get frightened and then become sad. At the same time, he would feel infuriated at his father's behaviour. Most days, he wanted to run away to a faraway place where he could breathe freely. He wanted to escape from his suffering and sorrow.

Today also he felt the same.

Ashim walked out of the house. He couldn't take it anymore. And there, in the darkness of the evening, he could see someone standing in the courtyard. He looked closely—it was Nirmal! Ashim took flight! He ran past Nirmal without saying a word. It was all so quick and sudden that Nirmal couldn't even catch a glimpse of Ashim's face!

Nirmal now understood what had happened to Ashim, even though they hadn't exchanged a single word.

Nirmal turned his head to look at the gate, but Ashim had already disappeared into the darkness.

5

The pain in Ashim's finger had alleviated a little, though the wound was still inflamed. Yet, Ashim had decided to go to the quarry today. After the scene his father had caused, he had felt listless. Perhaps because of his mental stress, he was also feeling tired physically. Yesterday's incident had extinguished the slender flame of hope that had been glimmering inside his heart. Amid all the despondency, Ashim had somehow managed to carefully preserve a little hope. He had thought that his dropping out of school might bother his father. That his going out to split stones for the sake of his family might move his father's stony heart was a futile hope. All his hopes were now dashed. He felt as if his father was pleased that he had dropped out of school and that now he had a right to his son's hard-earned daily wage to feed his bottomless addiction.

In a trance, Ashim continued to strike the stones to break them, and as the mound of broken stones grew larger, his fatigue increased and his body gradually became weak. However, his mind was elated because the more he worked, the more he earned.

But then suddenly, everything seemed meaningless again as his thoughts wandered—*how should I react to this unjust demand of Deuta?* He had been silent till now. Out of fear as well as out of respect. Because of his fear of his father, he never protested and, hence, his father's unjust demands kept escalating. Harassment and assaults on his mother kept mounting. Wouldn't it be proper and the right thing to raise his voice to rescue his mother from this pitiful plight? But then his father would certainly give him a severe thrashing! What would he do then? Would he then fight his own father? Ugh! How could he even think of such a horrid thing? Ashim's thoughts got enmeshed in a menacing maze of emotions. He felt trapped. After all, to not be able to respect one's father from the core of one's heart is a matter of great regret for a child. Ashim paused to reflect, for he couldn't turn to anyone; neither could he divulge his feelings to his mother nor could he share his thoughts with Nirmal.

But was that the truth? Couldn't he really divulge it to Nirmal? Isn't that why he had come to his house yesterday? Nirmal had never come to his home before. And what about his words to him the other day? 'Ashim, will you tell me what is bothering you?' These words, spoken in a gentle but deep voice, were still echoing in his ears. *Only an intimate, close friend speaks in this manner,* reflected Ashim. *Is it true then? Does Nirmal consider me to be a true friend? But then, he has also been a rival as far as studies are concerned. I had abandoned him at school the other day when I had run away and I did it again yesterday.*

Still, as Ashim remembered Nirmal's words of concern, he began to feel weak. The overwhelming emotions breached his restraint. His throat choked. His eyes became moist. His pent-up feelings spilled through his lips. He wanted to speak his heart out. He wanted to confide in someone. But how could he, when he had never done it before, speak about such things? It was easy to start a conversation about going out to harvest mangoes or to fish or to watch the jatra. But how could he share these deeply personal feelings?

Absorbed in his thoughts, Ashim was oblivious to the fact that his feet had carried him to the school gate. He stopped and noticed that the children were yet to arrive for the day's lessons. Every morning, when he walked to the quarry, the school campus would be quiet, and by the time he returned, it would be dark. So he always found the school campus soundless and without any activity. Ashim himself wanted to go past the school before official school hours started. He returned the same way after it had closed for the day, as he didn't want to run into any of his schoolmates. It would be too embarrassing for him. Still, he couldn't escape that lingering sadness whenever he crossed the school campus; a melancholic feeling would weaken him and, invariably, his pace would slow down.

Ashim looked around the campus intently. The school was still shrouded in the early morning fog. He turned to look at the bakul tree. All of a sudden, he felt as if he had left a very intimate friend behind when he gave up his school. When he had started to drift apart from the company of his schoolmates, it was this bakul tree that had become dear to his heart. Sitting under the tree, he used to brood over his life and its myriad problems. Even on the day the results were announced, he had sat there for almost half the day. He had come to feel for the bakul tree.

Ashim's thoughts now turned to the many events in his life. He recollected them, like the time when he had taken admission in class V and had won everyone's hearts within a few days. Everyone had appreciated him for being exceptionally sharp in mathematics. Mahendra master, the mathematics teacher, had once even patted his back affectionately in front of everyone, saying, 'Jewel! He is the jewel of our school!' And he had stood looking dumbfounded at his teacher with his mouth wide open like an idiot! Truth be told, he didn't know the meaning of the word 'jewel'! Realizing this, Mahendra master had gently rebuked him with a smile, 'Jewel means a gemstone, you idiot!' It was that very same teacher who had slapped him the other day, saying, 'You're ruined!'

Ashim could feel that his eyes had started to get moist. *These eyes!* Irritated, he rubbed his eyes forcefully before running towards the foot of the hill where the quarry was located.

6

Today, Ashim was very late for the quarry. When he got there, the rest of the boys had already begun work. Ramen, another daily-wage labourer who worked at the quarry, asked him, 'What happened, Ashim? Just a small hammer jab to your finger, and you are late to work today?' Ramen snickered.

'My dear Prince Charming! A physically delicate person such as you won't be able to hammer away at stones for long!' added Dipak, another co-worker, sniggering.

'What a butthead!' Ramen spat out.

Earlier, when Ashim was at the receiving end of these insults, he would turn red with shame. But that was not the case today. Today, he too retorted with bad language. But given his lack of experience in trash talk and the right intonation and body posture required to deliver it, the words, when they came out, sounded quite unwieldy and not quite right. Upon hearing Ashim's clumsy attempt

at street banter, the other boys burst into laughter. But
Ashim didn't let his nervousness show, and he too joined
in their laughter. This dissipated the tension, and Ratan
praised Ashim.

'This fella will soon learn our ways!'

'Oh, he was the bona fide jewel of our school, after
all!' Ramen remarked.

This startled Ashim. Suddenly, his spirit dampened.
Ramen used to be his classmate and was very poor in
mathematics. Quite often, Ramen used to be at the
receiving end of Mahendra master's ire. The boy would
regularly receive lashes from the master's thick, heavy
bamboo ruler. Then, one day, unable to bear the brunt of
this habitual corporal punishment and Mahendra master's
sharp tongue, Ramen dropped out of school. This was
long ago; when he was in class VI and Ashim was the
class topper.

Ashim became flustered because Ramen still
remembered Mahendra master's nickname for him—
jewel. The boy didn't want to be reminded of these
things from his former life, and he himself wanted to
obliterate these memories.

'Imagine! Baldy Mahendra called Ashim a jewel in
school. Jewel! Gemstone! And he called me an ox. Now
look, both jewel and ox are hammering away at stones
together!' Saying this, Ramen started laughing vindictively.

*So, Ramen still harbours resentment towards Mahendra
master,* thought Ashim as his mind started churning.
This also meant Ramen had taken the opportunity to
vent his own feelings. Perhaps Ramen harboured a sort

of bitterness against Ashim too. Looking back, Ashim
reasoned that Ramen must have felt awfully upset when
Mahendra master branded him an ox while hailing Ashim
as a jewel. At that time, Ashim was much younger and
didn't understand how praise and reprimand worked
like a double-edged sword. But now Ashim understood
from his own experience, how Ramen must have felt.
He instantly experienced hesitation and awkwardness
towards Ramen. But he decided—the past was the past,
and so be it! If they worked together here for some more
time, their relationship would organically fall into place
and the tension would dissipate.

'It's a difference of a few years,' Ramen continued.
'I dropped out of school early. As you were a jewel,
you dropped out later. That's it!' It was clear that the
antagonism which Ramen was carrying in his heart for
so long was now being unleashed with renewed vigour.

Ashim sat on his spot and decided not to respond.

At the quarry, they were seven boys who split stones
together. If Ramen had left school because of the beatings
from Mahendra master, Dipak had dropped out without
being beaten or bullied by anybody. And there was Ratan,
who didn't even get the opportunity to attend school.
There was only one thread that bound them together:
All of them were from impoverished families. Their lives
were as hard as the stones they had to break to eke out
a living. Their language was rough and straightforward.
Theirs was a different world altogether. A rock-hard
world. There was no luxury there to ponder over one's
feelings, nor was there any time to lament over losses.

Lifting the hammer, Ashim dealt a heavy blow to a stone. It split into pieces, which scattered in different directions.

*

Ashim's companions had left by now—measuring the crushed stones with a mustard-oil tin, Dibakar dada had given the workers their dues. Paresh, who was the owner of the stone quarry, had engaged Dibakar to run the quarry. Since Paresh was a contractor dealing in road construction and other sundry businesses, he had a lot on his plate that occupied his mind.

Ashim and his friends were young boys who did inconsequential jobs in the larger scheme of things. There was no need for them to come face to face with the owner of the quarry. All their interactions were with Dibakar dada alone. Ashim didn't feel the urge to know anything beyond that. And he didn't understand many things either. But he knew one thing for sure that the owner of the quarry was a rich and powerful man. A big shot. People feared Paresh a lot. Be it the Bihu celebrations or Durga Puja, the members and office bearers of the organizing committees always received Paresh warmly and often felicitated him on stage by garlanding him with a gamocha.

Ashim collected his wages but didn't head home. He felt reluctant to go there. Who knew, his father could be waiting for him right now? And if he went home, his alcoholic father would snatch his earnings to buy liquor, and the day's hard-earned money would go down the drain.

Ashim felt exhausted. He could have overcome his fatigue if he could go home and lie down on his cot. But for the time being, he put that thought away. Ashim decided to rest on a flat rock instead. What else could he do?

Gradually, the day was drawing to a close and darkness descended, intensifying in the areas around the hill.

Why had Deuta become such a person, his thoughts wandered. His father never used to drink earlier. This addiction grew over the last couple of years. And with it came a host of problems. For one, the villagefolk looked down upon drunkards. Ashim, too, didn't like people who drank endlessly. In fact, he was afraid of such people.

The night on which his father had entered home drunk for the first time, Ashim was terribly frightened. When he got a waft of the unfamiliar, pungent smell of alcohol, Ashim was nauseated and on the verge of throwing up. That night, Ashim's father muttered some incomprehensible words with a slurring tongue. That night, his father had also laughed out loud without any reason; his incoherent chatter had gone on endlessly. Ashim had found the entire scene bizarre. *Does it mean Deuta has turned into a bona fide drunkard? Do people now think of me as a drunkard's son?* Ashim felt very sorry that day for himself. He knew that gradually everyone in the village would come to know about this habit of his father. Including his schoolteachers. His friends. Perhaps one fine day, his father would be found lying by the road in a drunken stupor or would stagger along the road singing some out-of-tune song, followed by a group of hooting and jeering children. Perhaps his friends might also be part of the group! Ashim was terrified that day, worrying about these events, which he anticipated would occur soon. He couldn't even cry that night, although he was disenchanted to his very core. His mother had wept silently, lest the neighbours find out. Seeing their mother weep, Ajoli had cried too, at first silently, later sobbing loudly. Out of anger, Father had shoved her, shouting, 'Keep quiet!' Horrified, Ajoli stopped crying. But her grief didn't die. Instead, renewed anguish overwhelmed her tiny heart instantly. She had gasped for air and, in between breaths, let out small hiccups. Ajoli's heart had palpitated rapidly, and her face had turned blue. Seeing her in such a pitiful state, Mother had screamed in horror. And after a while, Ajoli lost consciousness and crumpled to the ground.

It was quite evident that for the first time in her life, Ajoli had faced such uncaring and insolent behaviour from her father, something so traumatic that it had resulted in her fainting. She had not been able to handle the tremendous surge of emotions upon seeing her once-loving father turning into an aggressor.

At one point, an unnatural silence hung over the house, as if someone had died. *Whose death? Death of what?* After pondering over it for a long time, Ashim realized that someone had actually died in their house—their loving father had died that night. This death stunned Ashim too. As in a house where someone had passed away and the hearth was abandoned, so too in their kitchen that night, the clay oven was not lit. None of them ate anything. Even little Ajoli.

That night, Ashim was too frightened to sleep beside his father in the same cot. So he waited. After his father had fallen asleep, he crept into bed quietly. In the dim light of the tin kerosene lamp, Ashim observed his sleeping father's face. He found it shrouded in mystery, just like the dim shadow projected by the tin lamp. It was as if he didn't recognize that person. Yet, he was the most familiar person in his life. It was his father who had earlier unveiled before him the mysteries of the world, one after another, with love, care and affection. He always thought of his father as a giant tree under whose shade he felt protected.

But this incident had taken place quite suddenly, like a raging storm. It had come quietly but had hit them with tremendous force.

And the giant tree had fallen instead of remaining rooted in the soil.

The man who was so near went so far away!

Away from everyone!

7

'Ashim!'
'Ashim?'
'Hey Ashim?'

Ashim jolted awake from his sleep and sat up on the flat rock bed. Intense darkness had descended upon the entire area. The birds, which had been chirping noisily a while ago, were now silent. In that profound silence, the word 'Ashim' had echoed across the entire hill. Ashim found it mysterious. Who would come in search of him at this hour, to this hill, tucked away in one corner of the village? He rubbed his eyes to remove the last vestiges of sleep.

'How can one sleep like this under the hill in this darkness? Aren't you cold?'

'Nirmal!' Ashim spoke. 'I–I fell asleep on the rock. I wasn't even aware.'

'Oh! You'll be aware all right when a tiger devours you,' said Nirmal with a smile.

'A tiger could very well eat you too, you know!' said Ashim, still surprised by the boy sitting before him. 'Weren't you scared to come to this place alone, and at this hour?'

'I arrived quite a while ago, actually.'

'Oh! Where were you?'

'I was sitting on the rock. Beside you. I didn't feel like waking you up.'

Ashim was quiet.

'Then it began to grow dark,' continued Nirmal. 'The surroundings became so very quiet, I started feeling a bit scared. That's why I woke you up.'

'If anyone finds out at your home, won't you get a scolding?' asked Ashim. He was aware of the rules prevalent in 'decent' households in the village.

'Come on, Ashim! My parents are not that bad,' exclaimed Nirmal. Hearing Nirmal's words, Ashim looked uneasy. Nirmal instantly realized that people in distress could be extremely sensitive, like Ashim seemed to be right now. And that one needed to be cautious while speaking to them. So, to lighten up the mood, he continued, 'Such a desolate place. Darkness all around . . . not a sound. It seems the jungle itself is shivering and being swayed by the breeze. Just like a scene straight out of a ghost story! You know, in such a scary setting, your snores sounded like a tiger's roar! If people hear it from a distance, they'll definitely take to their heels.'

Ashim erupted with laughter at Nirmal's comical description. He loved this banter with his friend. Earlier, Ashim had a kind of inhibition while interacting with

Nirmal. Perhaps, a sense of jealousy did rear its ugly head on occasion, but now, no such feelings clouded his mind. Rather, he wanted Nirmal to do well. He wanted Nirmal to do better than what he had already done.

At times, when Ashim mulled over the discord back home, it made his head feel heavy, and he felt a sort of breathlessness. In such a moment, he would look back and remember Nirmal's question of that evening at school after the slap, and a comforting feeling would envelope him. His gloomy heart would lighten up. At such moments, he felt like meeting up with Nirmal and chatting with him. He felt like talking to him about various things—myriad things that young chaps talked about. Most nights, when he would lay awake on his cot, Nirmal's words would pierce the thick veil of darkness and enter his heart's core, 'Will you tell me, Ashim, what is bothering you?'

Right now, Ashim felt like telling Nirmal what was bothering him. But he didn't know how to start talking about such things.

'What are you thinking?'

Ashim looked up, his thoughts returning to the present on being prodded by Nirmal's question. Engrossed in his own thoughts, he'd forgotten that he was not alone but was sitting with his former classmate. Nowadays, Ashim felt lonely even when he was with someone. He couldn't name or place this feeling and didn't know what exactly had happened to him lately.

'Nothing really,' Ashim responded casually.

'Hmm . . . why aren't you coming to school?' Nirmal breathed uneasily as he asked Ashim.

'Didn't you witness everything yesterday?' Ashim replied tersely, looking down.

Ah! 'That' incident was fresh in Nirmal's mind, too. He easily understood Ashim's indirect reply. *Oh no! I stumbled at the get-go!* Nirmal cursed himself internally. Indeed, he knew why Ashim had left school. But he had thrown the question Ashim's way only to break the ice. *Why can't he understand such a simple thing?* Nirmal didn't know of any other way to talk about such emotions. It was easier to play with friends or fight with them than to talk about these things.

'Will you come to school from tomorrow?' Nirmal asked Ashim softly.

'No.'

'Please come!' said Nirmal sharply, his patience wearing thin.

'No!'

'Come on, Ashim! Please rejoin the school!' Nirmal said softly, being mindful and emphatic this time.

'No, I won't rejoin school!' retorted Ashim harshly.

Damn! This halfwit doesn't even know how to discuss something, thought Nirmal to himself. Nirmal considered himself to be dumb, but he found Ashim dumber now!

Nirmal was not angry with Ashim for not coming to school, but for not having the tact to discuss or talk about things.

'But . . . why aren't you coming?' Nirmal asked again, a bit bitterly now.

'Can't you see?' Ashim lashed out.

'Yes, I can! You're sleeping on that cold rock bed, snoring! That's why you won't come to school?'

'Did I sleep the whole day?' asked Ashim incredulously. 'I only slept in the evening!'

Nirmal sighed. 'All right. Fine. Come to school in the day, then. In the evening, come here and sleep on this rock bed.'

'I'll work in the quarry and split stones during the day,' Ashim said quietly.

'And then return home in the evening and hand over your day's earnings to your father so he can drink even more than he already does?'

Ashim became silent.

Mustering a bit of courage, Nirmal continued, 'Tell me, what's the use of all this? All day long, you toil hard, breaking stones at the quarry. In the evening, your father snatches away your day's earnings! What difference does this hard labour make in your life? Your family's fortunes haven't turned by your hammering away at these stones. Rather, I feel it will destroy your family's well-being. If your father continues to get easy money like this, his addiction will get worse. And the more the liquor, the more the nuisance!'

After saying so much at once, Nirmal's fervour increased. Taking a deep breath, he spoke again, 'You will gain a lot if you don't work here, Ashim. You can go to school again. If you leave this job, your physical sufferings will end. And . . .' Nirmal stopped abruptly.

'And what?' asked Ashim, expressing his eagerness to listen.

Nirmal felt good now. Pointing towards Ashim's lacerated finger, he replied, 'You won't have to suffer all these injuries. Tell me, have you taken any medicine?'

Ashim nodded his head. 'I've applied bon xeuli juice on the finger. It'll heal automatically,' he said quietly.

'Right,' said Nirmal. 'So, tell me, will you come from tomorrow?'

'Come where?' asked Ashim, like an idiot again.

'To school!'

Ashim remained silent.

Nirmal knew the silence this time around meant that Ashim had not rejected his request straight away. It was a good sign.

'Will you rejoin school, please?' pleaded Nirmal.

Ashim sighed. 'My grades have deteriorated . . . and there are so many problems at home. What good will come from resuming my studies?'

'Look, Ashim, shying away from a problem doesn't help solve that problem,' saying this, Nirmal paused a little. He tried to remember whether he had read it somewhere, the line that he had just uttered.

He asked again, in a softer tone, 'Will you come?'

'Fine. I will think over it in the night,' Ashim replied in a serious tone.

Okay. This much is enough for today. As they say in the books, Rome was not built in a day! Nirmal reassured himself.

It was growing darker now. The two boys got up silently. The scattered glow of lamps coming from the houses that dotted the countryside made the scene appear intensely beautiful. The two could see the lights peppered here and there, around the foothill. They started walking towards their village, but neither of them said anything.

*

They had now reached Ashim's house and had halted at the gate. Just as they were about to part ways, Nirmal held Ashim's hand and gently said, 'I'll wait for you at school tomorrow.'

There was no reply from Ashim.

'Come on, Ashim. You know, when I don't see you in class, I feel very bad.'

Ashim remained silent.

'You know, I think of you all the time.'

Ashim remained silent.

Tears rolled down his cheeks.

Nirmal didn't see it.

It was pitch black.

8

Nirmal gave up hope. He had hoped that Ashim would come to school the next day. But Ashim didn't turn up. The morning assembly was over, and classes were about to begin. Still, stealing glances at the school gate, Nirmal waited eagerly in the veranda. But he knew, since Ashim didn't arrive by the time the assembly was over, there was no hope of his coming at all. After all, nobody comes to school after morning assembly prayers. Nirmal's heart was now filled with despair. Last night, Nirmal felt like he had made a breakthrough with Ashim. Perhaps, he now thought, after he had left Ashim at his house, maybe he had had a change of heart.

Sighing with a heavy heart, Nirmal decided to enter the class. He could not wait for Ashim anymore. By now, all the students had already occupied their seats. All this while, Nirmal had saved a place for Ashim by his side on the bench in the first row. In fact, he had not allowed anyone to sit there. It was just when Nirmal was about to enter the classroom that he saw Ashim enter through the school gate. Nirmal was elated! He wanted to shout out with delight! Nirmal saw Ashim stop under the bakul tree for a moment. He patted the tree trunk affectionately. Then, with slow and steady strides, he advanced towards Nirmal.

He came up to Nirmal and stood shyly.

'You've come!' Nirmal said.

Ashim nodded.

'Well done!' Nirmal smiled.

Ashim replied hesitantly. 'But . . . I have arrived very late.'

'That's okay. Try to come on time from tomorrow.'

'Umm . . .'

'Let's go and sit down,' said Nirmal eagerly.

Nirmal entered the classroom, followed by Ashim. None of the classmates other than Nirmal knew that Ashim had dropped out of school. At times, many a student remained absent for a week or two for various reasons, so everyone thought Ashim too had gone for some outing away from the village. Therefore, no one showed any curiosity when Ashim entered the room. Seeing this, Nirmal felt relieved.

However, Ashim felt a little embarrassed and decided to head towards the last bench. Just then, he saw Nirmal pointing to the seat he had saved for him in the first row. Surprised, Ashim stared at Nirmal.

'What are you looking at? Sit down!' hissed Nirmal.

'On the first bench?' asked Ashim, shocked. He had not sat on the first bench for over two years!

'Yes!'

Compelled by Nirmal, Ashim didn't have any option but to sit on the first bench.

'First period will be literature. Prafulla sir will take it,' Nirmal informed Ashim.

Ashim felt relieved. There was nothing that could make one scared of Prafulla sir.

'I haven't brought a single textbook! I have only managed to bring a notebook and a pen,' said Ashim.

'Don't worry. You can collect the textbooks and notebooks gradually. You can take my textbooks occasionally, too,' Nirmal replied in a comforting tone.

Just then, Prafulla master entered the class. He took the attendance. When the first roll number was called, Nirmal responded, as finally did Ashim. Just for a brief while, Ashim felt bad, but then as the class began, he started to feel more relaxed. And after some time, he began to feel good even.

I should rejoin school in earnest, thought Ashim.

In fact, he'd thought about everything till quite late last night. He had brooded over what Nirmal had said to him and eventually acknowledged that Nirmal was right. After much deliberation, he had decided he would return to school. Truth be told, he himself was not happy after dropping out of school. With each passing day, he became more and more upset. He'd noticed that, be it his habits, behaviour or speech, everything was becoming coarse. He could feel that. He had even started using obscene words. In fact, every night, lying on his cot, Ashim would brood over this. He'd become increasingly aware that he was turning worse, little by little. And in spite of knowing all this, he couldn't withhold or reverse the changes. It was as if everything was beyond his control. But now, perhaps because of Nirmal, he thought, his life would be saved from imminent destruction. Maybe he won't be able to excel in his studies again, but that was okay. At least he was in good company. The fond memories of his teachers' affection for him in his junior classes would keep him from ruin, he hoped.

Ashim now thought about Nirmal. He had come to like the boy very much as a friend. Whenever he met Nirmal or chatted with him, his mind became clearer and his sorrows seemed to lessen. He also felt inspired to be good. In fact, he even *felt* like studying—at least, as much as was possible given his limited resources. *If I keep on attending school regularly, I will get to meet Nirmal more often and talk to him even more*, Ashim had thought last night. He'd decided at one point, in the dark of the night, that he would come back to school. If needed, he would work at the quarry for a couple of hours after school. And on Sundays, he would work the entire day. But still, he would somehow make it to school.

But now in class, a new problem arose: Ashim didn't possess a single textbook of class X. He'd only somehow managed to fashion a notebook out of the unused sheets of the notebooks of class IX! It had taken him a considerable amount of time. It was because of this, in fact, that he had been late to school today. And the fact that he'd gotten up a little late in the morning as he'd remained sleepless till midnight, mulling over everything.

His mother was pleasantly surprised when she saw him with a notebook and pen in the morning. 'Where are you off to?' she'd asked him.

'School.'

This one word made his mother burst into tears. Ashim had read somewhere that people also cry when they are overjoyed. Perhaps his mother also felt happy.

Touching his forehead, his mother sobbed, 'You're doing the right thing, my son.'

He shrugged and then quickly moved away from his mother. *It looks so odd when grown-up people cry*, he thought.

The first period got over without any hassles. Ashim felt relieved. Nirmal also felt good. The fact that Prafulla master didn't treat Ashim harshly at all for being absent for a week came as a relief to both the boys. But it was the second period that they had to worry about. Because the second period was going to be a mathematics class taught by Mahendra master himself.

When Ashim found this out, he promptly took his notebook and got ready to retreat to the last bench. Just then, Nirmal grabbed his hand. 'No, no. Don't go. Stay here.'

But Ashim looked at him doubtfully. However, now Nirmal too felt that maybe sitting away from Mahendra sir would be a safer option.

'Okay, fine. Let's go,' Nirmal nodded, grabbing his books and notebooks.

Surprised, Ashim asked him, 'You're going to sit there too?'

'Yes.'

Shocked, Ashim kept standing there for a while till Nirmal poked Ashim's midriff with his bamboo ruler. 'Don't think too much. Let's hurry. Sir will arrive any minute now.'

They rushed and sat down on the last bench. No sooner had they taken their seats than Mahendra master entered the classroom. There was pin-drop silence in the classroom now. Even the sound of the boys' breathing could be heard.

Mahendra master looked at the entire classroom in silence. His gaze froze as he caught a glimpse of the last bench. Staring at Ashim, he said in a grave tone, 'Comet! So, you're back after a week!'

Nirmal's heart skipped a beat. Ashim started getting anxious too; it was as if he could no longer breathe. He recalled the sharp sting of the resounding slap that Mahendra master had dealt him a week ago.

Lowering his eyebrows, the teacher now glared at Nirmal. 'And you. Why are you clinging to him? Why are you sitting on the last bench?'

Nirmal didn't have any answers for that. He kept mum.

'Bah! That boy is already ruined,' he spat. 'And now, look at him, pulling down the entire class with him.'

Nirmal squirmed in his seat. He felt so terrible for Ashim that he couldn't even turn to look at Ashim's face. He continued to look down, as if examining his toes.

Ashim too was looking at the ground, his heart and head pounding.

All of a sudden, Mahendra master turned around and wiped the blackboard. As he was wiping it thoroughly clean, Nirmal pressed Ashim's hand and whispered in his ears, 'Don't get upset.'

But it was like Ashim couldn't hear anything. His mind was filled with utter shame, humiliation and despair. He could feel his heart constricting as his head started to become heavier. Physically, he started feeling sick—nauseous even. It seemed that the previous night's lost sleep now made his eyelids feel droopy. Throughout the period, not a single word of the topic that Mahendra master had taught had made any sense to him. An acute sense of despondency numbed his mind and body. It became so overwhelming for him that at one point, he started dozing.

Nirmal was at his wit's end when he saw through the corner of his eyes that Ashim had fallen asleep! Terrified, he poked Ashim with force, who now woke up with a violent jerk.

Ashim was unaware that he had dozed off! Now awake, he tried hard to keep his eyes open. If Mahendra sir saw him sleeping, it would spell doom for him.

Ashim tried to listen to the teacher's words intently. But a strange kind of fear started creeping into his mind. Time seemed to stand still. Ashim anxiously waited for the school bell to ring. His eyelids became heavy again. And after some time, no matter how much he fought it, his eyes closed.

Nirmal saw it instantly. And as soon as he moved his hand to prod Ashim, Mahendra master's hawk eye fell on them. It was as if he had been waiting for that very opportunity.

'You stupid boy!' he roared and rushed towards Ashim. Reaching the last bench, he shook in anger when he noticed that Ashim didn't have even a single textbook!

'Stupid! Idiot! Dimwit! First, you've appeared in school after one week. And then you have the gall to show your face with only one notebook? Who do you think you are? A college student?'

Ashim, now wide awake and scared, stood up silently with his head held down.

'Why are you dozing, you fool?'

Ashim didn't utter anything.

Mahendra master's anger escalated even more. 'Answer me. Why haven't you brought any textbooks?'

Ashim stayed silent.

'Answer me. Where have you been for the last one week?'

Ashim stayed silent.

'Sir . . .' Nirmal mumbled, wanting to say something, but the teacher just glared at him. 'You shut up; let this numbskull speak!'

Nirmal closed his mouth.

Mahendra master turned to look at Ashim again. 'Why don't you speak, you dimwit?'

Ashim stayed silent.

'Gah!' thundered the teacher. 'You're already ruined! Now you are pulling down Nirmal with you! Shame on you!'

Ashim stayed silent.

And Mahendra master's anger kept on surging. He spotted Nirmal's thick bamboo ruler, picked it up and addressed the other boy—

'Hold out your hand!'

Ashim held out his right hand.

One finger of his left hand had already been slashed by the hammer jab two days back.

Mahendra master dealt five lashes on the palm of Ashim's right hand with all his might.

He didn't cry.

He didn't withdraw his hand, either.

Mahendra master now spoke again—

'Hold out your other hand.'

He held out his left hand.

Another five lashes.

He didn't cry.

Neither did he withdraw his hand.

The sliced finger on Ashim's left hand ripped open and began bleeding. Drops of blood fell to the ground. Muttering angrily, Mahendra master went out of the classroom hurriedly. Terrified, the students remained silent.

Ashim with his lowered gaze saw that two of the pages of Nirmal's mathematics book had become wet with the blood dripping from his finger.

Turning towards his friend, Ashim said, 'Your book is damaged, Nirmal.'

Nirmal stayed silent.

He had started crying.

Ashim stepped out of the bench.

Nirmal realized something. He hurriedly spoke up, 'Don't get me wrong, Ashim!'

No, he won't get Nirmal wrong. Never. Ashim shook his head. He ran out of the room. He didn't even feel the need to pick up the notebook and pen.

Ashim ran past the gate. He didn't even stop near his beloved bakul tree.

Nirmal looked in the direction in which Ashim had disappeared. There were drops of blood along the way where he'd run. Nirmal's gaze now stopped at the doorway. And he was startled.

9

It was evening. Nirmal sat at his study table, but he couldn't concentrate. He was feeling horrible thinking about the incident that had occurred in school. The picture of Ashim's face flashed in his mind over and over. Nirmal could understand the intensity of pain that Ashim must have felt when Mahendra sir's lashes landed on his hands. What shocked him was the way in which Ashim's finger had bled, but still Nirmal didn't see any sign of suffering on Ashim's face. Ashim hadn't cried at all.

Nirmal noticed how much Ashim had changed in the last few days since he had left school, and this change was astonishing to him. Didn't he feel anything when others scolded or criticized him? *Perhaps he did*, Nirmal thought. *People cry when they are overcome by grief. But when that grief becomes overwhelming, perhaps they stop crying?* Even Nirmal cried before his parents when he was feeling overwhelmed. But he couldn't cry in front of other people. Perhaps it was the same with Ashim. Nirmal had a feeling that Ashim couldn't even cry before his parents. Perhaps he had moved away from everyone, and there was no one whom he could think of as his own.

Perhaps Ashim will never come to school again, Nirmal thought. He had managed to bring Ashim to school after so much persuasion! And he was so happy in the morning when he saw him walking in. But those ten lashes from Mahendra master had dashed all his happiness, all his hopes.

Ashim came to school with a glimmer of hope in his heart, and today, this too has been destroyed, Nirmal thought to himself, getting angry. *Why are adults so inconsiderate? Why don't they try to understand the struggles, the misfortunes which Ashim and others in situations similar to him suffer? Why didn't Mahendra sir and the other teachers try to understand the reasons behind the drop in performance of a brilliant boy like Ashim? Why didn't the teacher try to figure out the reasons that made Ashim stay away from school? Was it so difficult to understand why Ashim didn't have any textbooks? Why a person who could solve complex mathematical problems with ease, couldn't fathom such issues?*

Nirmal was angry, but he also felt guilty. He now reasoned it was because of him that Ashim had to suffer again. His lacerated finger had bled again—all because of him. Of course, the finger would heal after some time, but what about the humiliation that Ashim had suffered? Couldn't Mahendra sir or other adults like him feel that teenagers like Ashim or Nirmal too had a sense of self and self-respect? Couldn't they understand when they harshly scolded or punished teenagers like them in the presence of their friends and classmates, they would feel humiliated? And what was the outcome of the punishment? Would Mahendra master's beating keep Ashim from falling asleep during class? Would it help Ashim get his hands on the money to buy the textbooks he needed? Would he be able to solve all the mathematical problems in the world? Would he now attend school without fail? Not at all! None of these would happen! Rather, Ashim would leave school for good and become a dropout. Now, no amount of persuasion by Nirmal could bring Ashim back to school. Even Nirmal didn't feel like convincing and motivating his friend anymore when such belittling treatment awaited him back in school.

No matter how much Nirmal tried to study, he couldn't focus. The same thoughts kept niggling at him again and again. Why couldn't adults understand the problems of children? Adults think that children should play, study and be happy always, all the time. And whenever a certain Ashim didn't play, study or smile happily due to his circumstances, adults like Mahendra master got offended without trying to figure out the reasons behind this.

Nirmal cast a glance at the maths book in front of him on his study table. The splashes of blood on the two pages had dried up by now. But the stains were so deep that several pages underneath those two pages were soiled in blood too. It was so dark that a couple of lines in the upper portion on both sides of the pages had become illegible because of the bloodstains!

But Ashim hadn't even cried out when Mahendra sir punished him. He didn't even groan. He just said, 'Your textbook got damaged, Nirmal!'

Yes, his textbook had really gotten damaged. Nirmal shook his head in disgust. No, he won't study from this book again. In fact, he would ask his father to buy him a new one. If he used this particular book, the bloodstains in it would disturb his peace!

A person's mind is not like a textbook that can be replaced at will. Perhaps the mind is like a never-ending notebook where, day after day, new things get written. This notebook can never be changed, even if one wants to change it. At best, one can edit it. But the editing marks stay permanently too, just as they had remained today ·in the notebook of Ashim's mind. The boy had spent a sleepless night yesterday, where he wrote a sentence of hope in his mind's notebook but had to strike off that sentence in the morning. And the sentence that was ruled out, edited out, would remain as a dirty stain in the notebook. And even if Nirmal bought a new textbook, he would preserve this particular bloodstained one as a reminder of an unforgettably sad day.

Nirmal closed the textbook. He felt extremely restless. He felt like confiding in someone. But with whom could he talk? After all, he would not be able to express the storm that was raging in his mind. An inexplicable anger that now burned inside him made him restless. His forehead dripped with sweat. His head started aching.

Nirmal noticed the thick bamboo ruler lying on the table in front of him. He had made the ruler himself, with fondness and care, and had even etched his name on it: 'Nirmal'. But now, the ruler appeared to him to be a filthy and evil thing. There was no love or care left in it. Grabbing the ruler, he stormed out of the room.

Outside, Nirmal's mother was warming herself by a fire in the veranda. He went and sat next to her, and without saying a word, threw the bamboo ruler into the fire. His mother, who had seen her son make that very ruler with care, love and a lot of effort, was perplexed.

'What have you done? Why have you thrown this beautiful ruler into the fire?' she asked, surprised.

'Beautiful?' Nirmal spat out, disgusted. 'Can't you see that it's stained with blood?'

Startled, his mother looked at him, perplexed.

10

It was getting darker now. The faint haze had started to consolidate, with the pall stretching for miles. The occasional gusts of wind made his body shiver; still, Ashim remained seated on the veranda. He didn't feel like going inside the house. He shifted his gaze to his left hand. It was not bleeding now, but the injured finger had inflamed and become quite swollen. As the cold got worse, so did the pain. He winced. Today, Ashim hadn't applied the juice of bon xeuli on it. He hadn't even wrapped the wound with cloth. He didn't feel like doing anything at all. The bleeding had stopped on its own at one point. Perhaps the wound would begin to heal gradually. The pain might diminish. Whatever was going to happen would happen by itself. Ashim didn't have it in him to make anything happen. He just wanted to lie still, like a piece of log that had been thrown away into a corner, away from sight.

Ashim was unable to express what had occurred to him. He couldn't laugh, nor could he weep. He didn't feel happy, nor did he feel sad. He just didn't feel anything at all. *When paralysis sets in, one can't move or sense anything. Has my mind become paralysed too?* Ashim wondered.

He began to reflect on the events of the day. After that experience, there was no question of going to school anymore. *However, there is one positive outcome,* Ashim reasoned. Earlier, when he had walked past the school to work at the quarry, his heart had ached. It yearned to touch the bakul tree every time he saw it. He had an inexplicable bond with the glorious, hulking tree. At school, his classmates would want to engrave their names on the tree trunk. But Ashim never allowed anybody to do that. It was a special tree. A tree that had kept him company on the day of the result. A tree that had been with him when no one was there for him. Surprisingly, it was his father who had planted it. And this tree and the inanimate school building somehow occupied space in Ashim's mind.

Going forward though, he wouldn't dwell on the school or the tree, the teenager decided. Yes, the 'incident' with Mahendra sir was necessary to purge his mind. Yes, the unrest in his mind would be eased as the blood oozed out of his finger. His resolve to drop out of school was cemented by the incident. Ashim decided from this moment on he would no longer be conflicted, nor would he agonize over this decision. He now felt a strange sense of lightness in his being. He took a deep breath.

Just then—'How much have you earned today?'

Ashim lifted his head. His father was standing in front of him.

Upon hearing this, his mother, who was a little away from his father, glared at her husband.

'I didn't go to the quarry today,' Ashim replied.

'Why?' roared his father.

Ashim remained silent.

'Answer me—why haven't you gone to the quarry?' his father demanded angrily.

Ashim didn't reply. His mother replied for him, 'Leave him alone. He went to school instead!'

'What?' shouted Ashim's father, surprised.

Ashim's mother replied with equal force, 'Yes! And he'll go to school regularly from now on. He won't go to the quarry to break stones anymore.'

Livid with anger, the man howled. It seemed like he'd run out of patience. Picking up a bamboo stick lying on the veranda, he dealt a mighty blow on Ashim's bare back.

WHACK!

A sharp sound emerged as the lash slashed his back. Ashim felt as if his skin had been ripped off. Still, he kept sitting at the same spot.

His mother was distraught.

Another blow landed on Ashim's back. But still, he didn't utter a sound and stayed glued to the same spot. Immobile.

Enraged, Ashim's mother protested in anger and despair but to no avail.

Ashim's father again lifted the now-split piece of bamboo to strike the boy a third time. But this time, Ashim's mother rushed at him and snatched the stick away. She bent the stick with her hands and snapped it in two. She then threw the pieces into the courtyard with all the force she could garner. She stood in front of her husband and, looking into his eyes, thundered, 'Yes, he will go to school. He won't labour away at the quarry anymore.'

Ashim's father stood dumbfounded, startled by his wife's sudden rebellion.

The dark courtyard, now surrounded by a thick veil of fog, abruptly went quiet. Only the sound of the short, brisk breathing of Ashim's mother could be heard. A cat slunk in and silently settled down on the veranda, tucking her tail in between her hind limbs. A gust of cold wind wafted over the house.

'I won't go to school anymore. I will work at the quarry regularly from tomorrow,' Ashim said softly, looking at his feet.

His voice didn't hold any anger, anguish, or grudge. It was simply devoid of any emotions.

11

Nirmal's academic life was running smoothly. Since he had to appear for his matriculation examination this year, he'd been preparing well. They had exams every month nowadays and, in the two assessments that had taken place in the last two months, he had done well. The teachers in the school too had their hopes pinned on him and were expecting him to do well, and so Nirmal was going the extra mile to live up to their expectations.

It had been a while since the incident, but occasionally Nirmal did think of Ashim. And the moment he did, he would turn sad and bitter. He had done whatever he could, he would tell himself, but still he had failed to help his friend. So, whenever he remembered the unfortunate boy, Nirmal felt quite helpless.

Ashim, though, far away from academic concerns, became adept at breaking stones at the quarry. Nowadays, he could process large blocks of rocks in a very short span of time. Consequently, his earnings increased. On the other hand, his father's drinking habit got from bad to worse. As a result, discord at home grew manifold. His father's demand for money also increased. Therefore, the condition of the family didn't improve in spite of Ashim's increase in earnings. Ironically, the condition of his family reminded Ashim of the maths problem that he used to solve in class—the problem in which water flowed into the tank through one inlet and went out through another outlet.

The disturbing incidents at school gradually became distant memories for Ashim. Even if these stray memories occasionally muddled his thoughts, Ashim tried to push them away actively and not mull over them. Even his mother finally accepted the reality that he had left school for good. For better or for worse, everyone seemed to have accepted the change. His dropping out of school, his working in the quarry, his father's alcoholism and acts of nuisance—all these became familiar and the norm for everyone in the family.

And then one day, a new incident took place—an event no one in the family had anticipated. Nor could they come to terms with it.

12

Ashim was returning home from the quarry in the evening. Ratan and Ramen were with him too. From a distance, they could see a gathering of people in front of the school. Ratan and Ramen, thrilled to see something exciting happening, started moving at a brisk pace towards the crowd. Ashim, though not interested, just to keep up with them, also quickened his stride.

As they neared the front of the school, they could sense that something had happened under the bakul tree. People were congregating around the tree as they would during Durga Puja, in front of the idol. There was a festive atmosphere all around. People were hooting and whistling. There were yells and laughter all around.

When Ashim stopped near the school gate, the hullabaloo decreased. A hush fell. Everyone had noticed his presence. They made way for him, allowing him to walk forward. Just then, one or two people shouted, 'Make way for Ashim! Ashim is here!'

Ashim shot a glance at the people incredulously. *Why are these people giving me so much importance? And why are they making way for me to go towards my beloved tree?* As he walked, something struck him. The similarity of a house in mourning, where if any member living outside the village arrived at the gateway, the same thing would happen—people's murmurs would stop and they would make way for the member who approached the corpse. Ashim was now quite afraid, but he still advanced towards the bakul tree.

Ashim was stunned when he saw what had happened. He felt as if his breathing had stopped. His heart started to tremble. His legs started to shake. He felt dizzy and nauseated. His face and ears went red. For Ashim saw that the villagers had made his father kneel under the tree and forced him to hold his ears with his hands in punishment! Next to him was the village barber who was chopping off his father's hair haphazardly. His head was almost shaved but for a tuft of hair! Just as the barber grabbed the remaining tuft of hair to cut it off, someone shouted, 'Hey you! Look! Your son has arrived!'

But Ashim's father didn't lift his head. Seeing this, another person scolded him, 'Come on! Raise your head!' But Ashim's father kept his eyes to the ground. Just then, one bystander kicked his back, saying, 'See! This drunkard is finally ashamed!' A ripple of laughter ran through the mob.

Ashim staggered; he felt like crying aloud.

The barber now raised his father's head forcibly by pulling the tuft of hair he was about to cut. The son's eyes met his father's. Both lowered their heads simultaneously in humiliation.

Ashim felt like his lips were glued, his mind blank. He said nothing at all. He didn't know *what* to say, and to whom to say it, or even what to do. He didn't know anything anymore. He had been mutely observing the events of his life, like a third person, a mere onlooker. The one who didn't have power, intellect or any experience enough to control those events. All he could do was observe.

Ashim left the spot silently, leaving his father under the bakul tree in the hands of the village mob. With slow, heavy steps, he headed home.

*

At home, Ashim found his mother lying on the cot, with Ajoli nestled against her. There was not a single sound in the house. Ashim realized that his mother had already learnt about what had transpired under the bakul tree. It seemed like his mother's mental strength had drained away completely—a mental breakdown due to grief.

Feeling the same mental agony, Ashim threw himself on his cot.

The chasm between Ashim and his father had widened for quite some time now. Ashim didn't know whether it was his father who had drifted away from him or if it was he who had wandered away from his father. He knew only one thing—from the day his father had started drinking, he didn't feel at ease around him. Yet,

at one point in his life, his father used to be more like a
friend to him. They used to talk openly about things as
his father had an open, welcoming heart. They even used
to go fishing together, tend to the vegetable patch and
harvest vegetables together. Often, his father took Ajoli
and him to the hillside for a walk, and on their way back
home, he used to treat the children to hot samosas and
tea from roadside tea stalls. Their father might not have
expressed his affection for them by caressing them with
gentle touches or by calling them sweet nicknames, but
nevertheless they could feel the warmth of his love.

Looking at his father's state now, those earlier
memories seemed like dreams to Ashim. He found it hard
to imagine that those small celebrations were once real.
Ashim sighed; he didn't know when they had actually
started losing their loving father.

Ashim felt like sharing all these memories and
emotions with someone now. It was getting too much
for him to bear. But in whom could he confide?

There was one person who fit the bill perfectly, and
as soon as the thought occurred to him, Ashim could
hear the gently preserved words in his heart, 'Will you
tell me what is bothering you, Ashim?'

Yes, the one person in the world in whom he could
confide all his sorrows was Nirmal. But it had been ages
since he had seen his old friend. After that incident at the
school, they hadn't run into each other. Ashim's mind
raced: *Does Nirmal still remember me? Does he even wish to
meet me again? Has Nirmal heard about the shameful incident
that happened today under the bakul tree? What does Nirmal*

think of all this? Does Nirmal even have any words to offer as commiserations to me?

Just then Ashim heard a distant commotion. It seemed like a lot of people were walking while talking loudly. Ashim stayed alert and tried to make out what they were saying, frightened and hesitant. The sounds gradually got closer and shriller. Ashim's heart started to throb vigorously again.

It was already evening and the darkness had become all-pervasive. Today, his mother hadn't lit the earthen lamp at dusk, which was a ritual she adhered to conscientiously. Darkness had engulfed their house. In his heart, Ashim wished to let the entire world's darkness descend upon their house! He wished to let the darkness conceal them from everyone!

Ashim could now clearly hear the hoots and whistles and the shrieks and laughter of people. He could sense a procession coming towards their house. He heard someone shouting, 'See! This is the punishment we hand out to drunkards!' Following this loud catcall, a lot of people started shouting, 'Look! Look!' The procession now stopped at their gate and the people continued catcalling and laughing spiritedly.

In the midst of that all-pervading darkness, Ashim shut his eyes in shame.

Just then Ashim sensed that his mother was weeping. Yes, she was surely sobbing. At first, she was weeping silently, so others wouldn't know about it. However, the poor woman couldn't restrain herself for long. She let out a loud, mournful wail, thumping her chest and punching her forehead. Seeing this, Ajoli too started crying aloud.

Ashim pressed his tattered rag over both of his ears and closing his eyes, lay motionless on his cot.

13

It had started raining. At first, it had begun as a little drizzle, but now it was raining quite heavily. The downpour was so severe that the houses, even at a short distance, were not clearly visible. Selecting a book from his shelf, Nirmal got into bed. He perched himself on the side by the window. A cold wind made its way through the open screen and the potent vertical lines of rain struck the earth like sharp arrows, splattering mud. This much-anticipated rain had come after a long dry spell. The beautiful earthy smell of moist soil, petrichor, mingled in the breeze. In weather like this, it was fun to leisurely read a storybook, comfortably sitting by the side of an open window, while the rain poured outside. But today, Nirmal didn't feel like reading any story. He put the book aside and stared out of the window.

As Nirmal ruminated about the past, Ashim's face flashed in his mind.

Nirmal hadn't met Ashim for a long time now. He knew very well that if he himself didn't make an effort, he wouldn't be able to meet Ashim. Since that incident at school, Nirmal had been feeling a little guilty too. After all, Ashim had agreed to come back to school only at his insistence.

Why couldn't I say anything that day, he now thought. When Mahendra master had scolded Ashim, Nirmal had tried to say something, to explain, to reason. But the teacher was so red with anger, he hadn't even given him the chance to intervene. What should Nirmal have done that day? What would have been the right thing to do? Should he have ignored Mahendra sir's harsh words and narrated what Ashim had to endure at home? Should he have protested after he saw the ruthless beating? Maybe then, he would have been called a disobedient student too, a student who had gone astray, thought Nirmal. Perhaps the teacher would have complained to his parents for talking back in class and arguing with a teacher. *But then Ashim's life would have been saved from this mindless destruction!*

Nirmal felt very helpless. And as he was thinking about all this, another recollection interrupted his chain of thoughts.

A new teacher had joined their school. His name was Anubhav. The day he joined their school, an incident took place.

The headmaster of their school had accompanied the new teacher to their class and introduced him to the students, 'He is your new teacher who has come from a far-off place just to teach you. Welcome him with a warm namaskar.' All the students stood up and greeted the new teacher. The students felt that there was something in the smile of the teacher—a grin which could make one feel easy and comfortable in his company.

'Right! I've brought him to make introductions. Classes are yet to be allotted to him. Now, I request Anubhav master to take this period.' Saying this, the headmaster left the room.

The new teacher introduced himself again with a smile, 'Hello students. I am Anubhav, and I will be teaching you mathematics.'

Nirmal and other students were shocked. They were already in class X, but for the first time in their student life, they had encountered a maths teacher who could smile! Was that even possible?

After introducing himself, the new teacher now earnestly started talking to the children. He not only asked everyone their names and where they lived, but he also tried to learn about their hobbies! Quite obviously, everyone was excited and intrigued. And just when this was happening, the incident took place.

A member of the non-teaching staff marched into the classroom. A student of class VI accompanied him, and he was carrying an answer sheet in his hand. The boy was looking downcast and was visibly upset.

Addressing the new teacher, the non-teaching employee said, 'Sir, you won't believe what this student has written in the Axomiya paper! If you hear it, you'll roll on the floor with laughter!'

The student hung his head in shame—red in the face.

The man continued, 'As punishment, the Axomiya teacher has asked him to read his answer aloud before the students in every class!' he added in a mocking tone. 'He has already read it before the students of classes VII, VIII and IX. Everyone who heard it found it hilarious. Now it's class X's turn to hear him read aloud his ridiculous answer.'

Nirmal could see the smirks and grins on the faces of his classmates. Everyone was gearing up for a laugh. Nirmal turned to look at the unfortunate student. His face had acquired a sickly pallor, burdened at once by terror, disappointment and humiliation. For a second, Ashim's face flashed in Nirmal's mind. Perhaps this boy's fate too would be like that of Ashim. This embarrassment would force him to leave school too! Would he be able to bear this almost-violent public humiliation? With apprehension, Nirmal looked towards the new teacher. He noticed that the new teacher was looking at the boy with a lot of affection.

The non-teaching employee instructed the student roughly, 'Read now!'

The little boy readied himself to read aloud.

Just then, Anubhav, the new teacher asked him softly, 'What's your name, little one?'

Looking down, the boy stuttered, 'A–Atanu.'

'Nice name!' After a pause, the teacher asked him again, 'Okay, Atanu, tell me, what was the question in the exam?'

'W–Write any story from your textbook in your own language,' Atanu replied in a low octave.

'Okay. Now read out what you have written.'

Atanu was a bit hesitant. The teacher encouraged him, 'Don't worry. Just read.'

Atanu started reading the answer out loud. He had written the story in the colloquial or typical conversational style in which people in that region conversed at home. On hearing a couple of sentences written in informal speech, the students as well as the employee accompanying the boy burst into laughter. Nirmal noticed that the teacher did not laugh at all. Rather, his facial expression became serious.

'Don't laugh, students. Atanu, you read on,' the teacher gently prodded the boy, who had now stopped reading out of embarrassment. Extremely humiliated, tears had started streaming down his cheeks.

The boy now started reading the story in a quivering voice. Anubhav, the new teacher, listened to his narration very intently. On seeing him don a serious look, the students were shocked but, imitating him, started listening to the story silently as well. Nirmal smiled on the inside, for he found the narrative interesting since it acquired a new flavour in informal, everyday speech, spouting from Atanu's lips. The story sounded a bit strange, for sure, but it was also immensely enjoyable and unique.

After some time, Atanu finished reading his story.

The teacher remarked, 'Well, that is quite well written.'

Atanu, who was standing there with his face downcast, couldn't believe the teacher's words. Nirmal's classmates couldn't either! Everyone, including Atanu, thought that the teacher was pretending to be serious and would break into laughter any minute.

Anubhav master spoke softly, 'I am saying this in all honesty; you have constructed the story very well. You were asked to write a story in your own language. You haven't memorized the story from your textbook and reproduced it verbatim but have written it as you would normally speak—not formally.'

Everyone, including Atanu, stared at the teacher's face in disbelief.

Anubhav master smiled. After a pause, he said again, 'If I were your Axomiya teacher, I would have given you ten out of ten.'

Atanu suddenly started sobbing upon hearing the teacher's words of praise. Nirmal noticed that the new teacher's face had become unusually compassionate. The teacher then got up and wiped away Atanu's tears. The class was shocked, as was the staff member. For the first time in their lives, they had witnessed a teacher wiping away a student's tears.

And foolish little Atanu started crying even more.

Nirmal's eyes became moist too.

The staff informed the teacher, 'The Axomiya teacher has awarded him a big zero.'

Hearing this, the new teacher replied, 'I'll speak to him.'

Then, he left the classroom holding Atanu by his hand and talking to him along the way. Nirmal and his classmates kept staring into space, speechless.

*

Recalling that day's incident, Nirmal became emotional. He realized that his eyes had become moist, just like that day in the classroom. He knew in his heart that Ashim too needed that kind of love and compassion from a teacher. In fact, he needed it a great deal more than anyone else but, unfortunately, would never receive it.

Nirmal looked towards the horizon in despair. It was still pouring buckets outside.

14

The rain showed no signs of letting up.

It's not possible to break stones in this rain, Ashim thought. He got up from under the tree. His companions had left before the rain had started pouring heavily. Only he had stayed back alone. After all, what would he do going home so early? He didn't feel like staying at home at all! The atmosphere in the house had changed a lot after their father had been paraded in the village with his hair chopped off, for creating nuisance in the village in an inebriated state. A weird atmosphere now prevailed instead. The family members hardly talked to one another.

His father didn't speak to anyone in the house unless there was a pressing need. And then there was his mother, who carried out the daily household chores silently. The environment in the house was just like that of a patient's room in a hospital—it appeared calm and quiet from the outside, but a constant state of anxiety prevailed inside.

Ajoli, Ashim's little sister, had suffered the most in this unfavourable environment. She loved to have fun, to skip about, and to generally enjoy her childhood in a lively way. Now, seeing everyone's gloomy faces in the house, Ajoli had also turned sombre overnight. It was evident from her demeanour that she was suffering a lot. At times, Ashim felt she was like a plant growing in a shady, dark corner of a garden. A plant growing in a dark and damp place bends towards sunlight, seeking warmth. The stem of the plant doesn't grow straight. *Would Ajoli's life stay simple and straight now? Wouldn't her life take a different turn, seeking some light and warmth?* Ashim wondered. He also pondered whether he himself was a sickly plant growing in the damp.

And what of their father? Was he also a plant deprived of light? A plant which was decaying day by day because of the lack of light and heat. What was that darkness which had engulfed him? Did he make an effort to dispel that darkness? Ashim didn't know the answers to any of these questions.

The distance between Ashim and his father had increased exponentially, with each passing day. One can feel love and affection for someone till one remains at a certain distance. Perhaps, even in order to feel anger or hatred, one needs to be within a certain limit. But when someone moves beyond that distance or limit, perhaps one cannot even feel anger or hatred towards that person. Perhaps Ashim and his father had crossed this threshold, and the boy had lost the ability to feel any kind of emotion towards his father.

But that fateful day, Ashim had noticed one thing: how his domineering and aggressive father had become docile in front of the villagers. On that fateful day, the individual who had been tormenting Ashim, his mother and Ajoli at home found himself compelled to kneel under the bakul tree, helpless and mute. And when Ashim's eyes had met his father's, he had seen immeasurable humiliation in them in those few seconds. Suddenly, just by recalling this particular bit, Ashim felt a surge of empathy for his father.

Ashim's mind went through the events of the night once again. He could see everything clearly. Overwhelmed by immense mental and physical stress, the disgraced man had returned home after midnight on that day, on the verge of breaking down. He lay down on the rough earthen veranda of the house in pitch dark and had remained there like a piece of wood the entire night. He had not wanted to make his presence felt; he had not let out a single groan nor had he moved his body in the slightest. For three days thereafter, he had relegated into one corner of the house, hiding. He had not eaten anything. It was clear that he had felt immensely degraded by the punishment meted out to him by the village mob. Maybe an ounce of shame was still left in the man after all, Ashim had ruminated. Perhaps, the punishment by the village folk had affected that last remaining ounce of dignity.

On the third day, he had overcome all embarrassment and had again resumed his alchoholism. This time, it was during the day. He had returned home, hurling abuses loudly at the villagers along the way. Not an iota of shame shrouded his face that day. In fact, it had been replaced by severe mulishness, so much so that his face had taken on a permanent stern expression.

The problems in Ashim's home now grew insurmountable. Earlier, his father used to drink only at night. But now it was round the clock. Ashim's mother was hit the hardest by this. All the pent-up anger and frustration at not being able to get back at the villagers now made his father release all his anger on her. Being at the receiving end of her husband's temper, the poor woman would groan in pain all night long. And from a distance, Ashim would watch this without any emotion. He became a mute spectator. He couldn't comprehend what was happening and why it was happening—whenever the discord escalated in his house, his hammer jabs at the quarry became intensely forceful and frequent and the mound of broken stones grew taller.

*

Ashim was shaken awake from his reverie. He heard a loud sound, as if someone was running through the jungle. Ashim squinted to see a huge boulder rolling down the hill rapidly after being dislodged from its place. As the boulder rolled, it was crushing everything in its path—trees, both small and big, along the way. It seemed that the bird's nests in the trees had been destroyed, too. For a flock of birds were flying helter-skelter, screeching in panic. But because of the relentless rain, these birds couldn't even fly properly. The huge boulder finally stopped at the foot of the hill. As if it were a baby separated from the mother's bosom, it writhed violently in agony before finally ceasing to breathe.

Ashim looked up at the hill. It had changed a lot before his very eyes. Earlier, it had been covered with big rocks and wild trees. It was said that people even used to hear the roars of tigers there at night. That hill, once lush with vegetation, was now stark and bare. The tree cover had gone down drastically. The quantity of rocks had also reduced, and now caverns spotted the hillside. As a result, whenever it rained, the soil in the hill came loose, and the rocks hanging above those caverns lost their grip and came rolling down. Ashim turned to glance at the road below the hill. The rainwater mixed with the red soil of the hill had washed the road with a red tint. It was as if the hill had vomited blood.

Is the hill suffering from some disease? Ashim thought. He sighed. Yes, once the hearts of his father and mother too used to be filled with love, care and laughter. Back then, it was as if each of them were a hill covered with lush vibrant greenery. But the grip of the soil in those hills got weakened. Then came the landslides; and love, care and laughter got uprooted one after another. And finally, everything became barren. Were his parents also suffering from some disease like the hill? And what was it? Did it have a name?

Ashim moved out from under the tree. He walked towards the dislodged boulder amid the relentless rain. Once he reached there, drenched, he gently touched the stone with affection. He began to feel as if the boulder was his sister Ajoli or as if it was he himself, as if the hill was his father and mother and that the homeless birds flying here and there were their lost laughter, love and care.

Ashim stood there, soaked in the rain, within the desolate ambiance surrounded by the hill. All alone.

15

Through the window, Nirmal saw a figure enter their gateway, drenched in the rain. *Ashim! Ashim had come to their house!*

Ashim stepped into their courtyard. Delighted, Nirmal jumped out of bed shouting, 'Ashim, Ashim!' and rushed to the veranda.

'Come, Ashim. Come onto the veranda. Why are you getting soaked in the rain like that?' Nirmal shouted over the pitter-patter without stopping to catch his breath.

Ashim didn't reply but quietly walked towards the veranda. Nirmal was astounded as he observed Ashim closely. All his excitement and delight at meeting his friend after a long time vanished. Ashim's threadbare clothes were completely drenched and his wet hair stuck to his thin body. His eyes looked sunken, as if they were placed inside hollow pits. He had become extremely skinny. His appearance conveyed the impression that he had been suffering from a chronic ailment. Ashim looked like he had aged! This was no teenager! This Ashim was unfamiliar to Nirmal. This boy was not the Ashim whom Nirmal had met in school. Ashim had changed a lot in a span of only three months. Nirmal kept staring at his friend, astonished.

Ashim felt a bit uneasy. He asked Nirmal with a sad smile, 'What are you looking at so keenly?'

Somewhat unnerved, Nirmal just replied, 'Come inside.'

'No need for that, Nirmal,' said Ashim. 'It will get dirty. I am anyway drenched to the bone.'

Nirmal grabbed a gamocha that was hanging on a clothesline in the veranda and held it out to Ashim. But the boy didn't take it. He just said, 'No need for that too. My clothes will eventually dry by themselves.'

Both of them remained silent. The rain was yet to let up. The wind was howling and blowing constantly. What could Nirmal say to Ashim? He had a lot to say and had a lot to ask, too. Somehow, though, he couldn't articulate anything. In order to lessen the uneasiness, he said, 'So . . . umm . . . what brings you here, Ashim?'

Ashim couldn't say anything in response. Why had he come to Nirmal's home? Did he miss his old friend? Did he feel like returning to his school days, back into Nirmal's company?

'How are your studies going on?' asked Ashim instead.

His question created a kind of restlessness in Nirmal's heart. He became teary-eyed.

'Well . . . everyone in the village has great expectations from you that you will do well in the exam.' Pausing briefly, Ashim added, 'I do too.'

Nirmal's eyes began to well up. In order to hide them from Ashim, he turned to the other direction. 'A new teacher has joined our school,' he shared.

Nirmal didn't notice any excitement in Ashim's demeanour, so he repeated, 'The new teacher is very different. He is very loving towards all of us.'

Hearing this, something strange happened. Ashim's face wore an expression of pain. His lips trembled, and he became restless. Nirmal saw that water droplets were rolling down Ashim's cheeks. He wasn't sure whether those were drops of rain or tears. And, all of a sudden, drops of water were flowing down Nirmal cheeks too. Those were tears surely, as Nirmal hadn't got wet in the rain at all! Ashim would know it if he were to look directly at Nirmal's face.

Ashim was surprised to see Nirmal stepping off the veranda onto the courtyard. As he started to get wet in the rain, he extended his arms wide open.

What have I said that has made Nirmal get drenched in the rain? Ashim kept observing the scene in astonishment.

16

Ashim walked home in the heavy downpour. He'd never had the chance to use an umbrella. They didn't even have an umbrella in their house. Whenever the need arose, they used a big leaf of arum in place of an umbrella. Today, Ashim didn't feel like holding an arum leaf over his head. He just walked in the pouring rain for a long time. He didn't know what had come over him; he just wanted to soak in the rain. Maybe it kept his restless and turbulent mind calm.

As he walked, Ashim had no idea that Mahendra master was approaching from the opposite direction. The incessant rain made it difficult to make out anything in the distance. Ashim came face-to-face with his former teacher and he had no choice then but stop. Even now, he felt quite nervous.

Mahendra sir called out to Ashim in a rough voice, 'Why are you loitering like a cow in this rain?' As he spoke, the teacher sneaked a peek at Ashim's left hand with the corner of his eyes. Ashim didn't notice this as he was standing there, with his eyes on the wet ground. Mahendra saw that Ashim's thumb had healed, but a scar was there.

The sense of humiliation had still not left Ashim. Perhaps if his thumb had not cracked and bled in the incident three months ago, maybe he wouldn't have felt so much embarrassment even now.

Suddenly, a thought struck Ashim. He was not at school anymore and didn't need to heed any remarks from his former teacher! And so he took flight.

Mahendra master was bewildered. He stood there, watching Ashim sprinting. On regaining his composure, he raised his right hand and shouted, 'You'll slip, you idiot!'

Mahendra master was not sure whether Ashim heard his warning or not, as a thunderclap drowned out his voice.

17

Anubhav master was feeling quite uncomfortable. He never expected to get entangled in a difficult situation within one week of joining the school. When he had seen Atanu's face, he felt a deep sense of empathy for the boy. On seeing the little boy's terror-stricken face mingled with the fear of disgrace, Anubhav earnestly felt like giving the little boy some respite. But in doing so, he hadn't had the slightest intention of maligning a senior teacher. At the same time, his conscience had not allowed him to accept the punishment given to little Atanu by the Axomiya teacher, Prashanta master.

Anubhav didn't even support the idea of awarding the boy a zero for that particular question. And he had tried to convey the same to Prashanta sir without any malice. But the senior teacher had not shown any inclination to either listen or discuss the matter. Rather, his face had taken on a kind of uneasiness at this unsolicited intervention from the newcomer. Perhaps he would have preferred to learn what had transpired from the non-teaching employee who had accompanied Atanu. But then, who knew how the employee would have narrated the incident in the first place? Maybe he would have added some spice to the story. Anyway, it was quite clear: if Prashanta master could not accept anything with an open mind, then even if he got to know what had actually happened, it would make him uncomfortable.

Possibly the issue has become very serious internally, Anubhav mused. A little while ago, Headmaster Sanatan asked Anubhav to meet him after school hours to discuss an urgent matter. Just before that, Mahendra sir had met Anubhav alone and had asked him, 'What happened in your class on Saturday?'

Anubhav had narrated the incident, after which Mahendra sir had asked him a couple of relevant questions and listened attentively to what he'd said. However, without saying anything further, he left the spot. His face had donned a serious look. Anubhav had understood that Mahendra sir would now approach and listen to the version of Prashanta sir, followed by the version of the employee to get a wholesome perspective of the event.

Anubhav figured the teachers in the school respected Mahendra sir and held him in high esteem. Added to that, the man also had a good name in the village and was regarded as an exceptionally good mathematics teacher in the area. Mahendra sir also seemed to be a trusted aide of Headmaster Sanatan, as the man would make many decisions on the advice of the mathematics teacher. Anubhav reasoned perhaps it was Headmaster

Sanatan who had given Mahendra sir the responsibility of investigating the matter.

But Anubhav wasn't sure what implications the ensuing events would have in store for him. He knew that Mahendra sir liked him. When he first joined this school, the man had helped and guided him in every aspect, even while he was searching for rented accommodation.

But Mahendra sir was also a strict disciplinarian. How could Anubhav forget the incident that happened on the first day? The students feared Mahendra sir more than they loved or respected him. He was known for giving out the strictest of punishments if students failed to solve mathematical problems, disobeyed rules and regulations, or didn't maintain discipline.

Calculating all these things in his head, Anubhav was almost sure now that Mahendra would side with Prashanta on this issue. *Why only Mahendra sir, certainly the rest of the teachers would also be against me now,* he thought. Anubhav knew that he was too new in the system and that his relationships with others were only at the nascent stage, and that his familiarity with everyone was yet to take the shape of friendship to garner any sympathy from his colleagues.

Suddenly, Anubhav felt as if he was still an outsider in the school. And perhaps after the meeting today, he would move farther apart from his peers. A sense of forboding filled his mind, thinking this.

The matter was not about Prashanta's or Anubhav's win. It was actually a conflict of two approaches to teaching. It was a clash of two schools of thinking.

Prashanta sir's approach reflected the traditional approach to teaching that was prevalent in the school till now. Maybe it was a reflection of the entire education system! On the other hand, Anubhav's approach challenged this prevailing, conventional method.

It was quite apparent from Anubhav's mannerisms and teaching style that he had some already-formed opinions and reflections regarding the current education system and that he was apprehensive about it. But he was quite clear: He had new methods of teaching, and he wanted them to clash with the older ways.

A clash of ideologies.

Anubhav was also clear that through this clash, he wanted to refine and evolve his own ideas.

Since all the teachers would be present in today's meeting, the currently prevalent approach to teaching would be accepted by all and would find favour with the larger group. There was no doubt about it. However, not only was the meeting undoubtedly important for Prashanta and himself, but it was far more critical for the students in the school and even more important for the generations of students to come. And however much someone might try, he wouldn't allow the differences of opinion to come down to a personal level. He would openly present his thoughts and ideas before everyone. And he would do so earnestly and with utmost honesty. He wished that at least everyone would deliberate on the issue. And while he was at it, he would share with his colleagues the thoughts brewing inside his mind—about the current education system and the issues plaguing it.

All he wanted was an honest and open debate. Thereafter, whatever was to happen would happen. There was no point in thinking about that now, ahead of time.

Anubhav felt as if a heavy burden had been removed from his heart as he resolved to present his case earnestly to the teachers of the school.

18

After school was over, teachers trailed into the common room, one after the other. There was seriousness in everyone's face. No one was talking. If someone's gaze met Anubhav's, they either tried to turn their faces the other way or gave him a weak smile. However, as they were overcast with worry, their smiles couldn't reach their eyes or light up their faces. It was evident that everybody was aware of the matter already. An uneasy calm hung heavily in the air in the common room, which was completely out of the ordinary.

Addressing everyone in the teachers' common room, Headmaster Sanatan started to speak, 'Our Prashanta has lodged a minor complaint about being offended by one of Anubhav's remarks. I thought we should discuss it as a group.'

Anubhav understood that the headmaster was trying to make things easy. After a pause, Sanatan continued,

'First, Prashanta will tell us why he is offended by our new teacher's actions.'

On cue, Prashanta master stood up to speak. Anubhav noticed Prashanta's nostrils flaring up and down. It seemed as if anger was brewing inside him. A sense of insult seemed to have clouded his face.

Although everyone in the room was aware of the matter, still, Prashanta narrated the incident. His narration was brief and precise: Atanu, a boy from class VI, had written a story in the exam in colloquial speech. Prashanta had given him a zero for this. And as punishment for writing such an outlandish answer, Prashanta asked Atanu to read aloud his story in each class—from class VI to class X. This took place last Saturday, that is, the day before yesterday. And so, when Atanu had entered the class X room, this new teacher was present there. He had praised Atanu in front of everybody, saying that the boy had written the story quite well. He had even commented that had he been the teacher concerned, he would have awarded Atanu ten out of ten and not a zero. In his closing argument, Prashanta added, 'With this kind of brazen behaviour, Anubhav has insulted me openly and challenged my authority in front of the students. He has tried to give the impression that he is far superior to me as a teacher. And that I am stupid . . . A dumbhead!' The last words spewed out in anger, the pitch of his voice rose in agitation. Prashanta was now gasping for breath.

'I am feeling humiliated. Utterly humiliated,' with these words, the teacher finally sat down.

Headmaster Sanatan now looked towards Anubhav. 'Is it true? Is Prashanta telling the truth?'

Anubhav nodded. 'True. Completely true!' He acknowledged the matter simply, without any protest.

'Hmm . . . would you have really given Atanu ten out of ten for that answer?'

'No, sir.'

Anubhav's reply stirred up a hornet's nest. A chaotic din spread across the room.

Prashanta got up from his chair, huffing in anger. 'Then why did you say you would award Atanu ten marks? To insult me?' he spluttered.

Even the headmaster was riled up! However, he managed to suppress his anger. After all, he was the senior-most teacher in the school and was going to retire next year. To display his anger in public would be unbecoming for such a man! 'What would you have given Atanu if not ten or zero?' In spite of his best efforts, the headmaster's voice sounded a bit harsh.

Anubhav replied calmly, 'Eight.'

Everyone went silent for a few seconds; they needed some time to stomach Anubhav's reply. Startled by his unabashed answer, the headmaster did not ask him any more questions and just kept looking at his face.

'You would have awarded him eight marks? You said that you would give him ten on ten,' Mahendra master broke the uneasy calm. 'Can you please explain why you would even give him an eight?'

It seemed that Mahendra had expressed what was on everyone's mind.

'Yes, I would have definitely awarded Atanu eight marks,' said Anubhav calmly. 'Why wouldn't I give him ten, you ask? Well, although he wrote the story in colloquial, everyday speech, some of the spellings of the words used did not match their pronunciation. Therefore, I wouldn't have awarded him ten marks. However, coming back to the story, Atanu read a beautiful story in conversational, informal speech. I really liked it when I listened to it. That's the reason I told him that I would award him ten marks. He was already crushed by the unbearable shame and humiliation he had to bear, going from class to class and having to repeat the story over and over again. The punishment imposed on him was unbelievably cruel. There is no way a child that age can handle such mental trauma. His self-confidence took a beating . . . being humiliated again and again in front of his seniors and friends. His posture, his voice and his expressions reflected his resignation and complete lack of self-confidence. I was moved by his plight.'

The common room became silent.

'But didn't your action humiliate Prashanta too?' Sanatan asked.

'If he felt humiliated, I would be hurt too. Actually, I had tried to talk to him about the matter . . . so he wouldn't take it the wrong way and feel hurt.'

Everybody looked towards Prashanta, who now nodded his head slowly.

Anubhav noticed the initial stern expression on Prashanta's face had softened to some extent. The other teachers were also listening to him attentively.

They seemed a little calmer, and no one was trying to chastise him.

'If I were in his position,' continued Anubhav, 'I, too, would have felt disrespected. But we adults can sort out our issues through discussions. We can distinguish right from wrong. Because of our age, our experience is vast. We can also lessen our suffering that is caused by someone's insults. But boys of Atanu's age are very fragile. It's a different matter there. Insults make them suffer internally, intensely. That day, when I saw the excruciating suffering and humiliation in Atanu's eyes, I was convinced that he would not be able to get out of that trauma easily. The way he lost his self-esteem, his self-respect, he would not be able to regain his confidence again. With time, as he grows up, he will be a citizen of this nation. Perhaps he would become a citizen devoid of any self-confidence. And his lack of confidence would be reflected in every task that he would undertake—be it while discharging his duties as a citizen of this nation or in fulfilling his duties as a member of his family.'

'Who knows, he could even stop attending school altogether.' Mahendra sir uttered these words involuntarily, all of a sudden, interrupting the monologue.

Anubhav glanced at the mathematics teacher. He was looking downwards, fidgeting with the end of his dhoti. Anubhav then turned to face the headmaster. He saw that the older gentleman was keenly observing Mahendra sir. It was quite evident to Anubhav that there was a deep bond between the two senior teachers; one could easily perceive what was going on in the other's mind, and Sanatan could understand what was left unsaid.

'That is why,' Anubhav continued, 'I thought that this ten- or eleven-year-old boy should get as much of a boost in his confidence as possible, in that moment, in that environment, to assuage some of the humiliation he had endured during that time. And so, I praised him a lot, even a little more than he deserved. At first, he didn't show any reaction, as he didn't trust me or my words of appreciation. Perhaps, he thought what I was saying was also a new way of ridiculing or insulting him. But when he realized that I was actually praising him and appreciating his work, he burst into tears.'

The room went silent. Nobody uttered a single word. Headmaster Sanatan and Anubhav noticed that Mahendra was becoming even more restless. 'Oh, something has gotten into my eyes,' he said all of a sudden, standing up abruptly while rubbing his eyes. Then pretending to call out an employee named Haricharan loudly, he left the teachers' common room. Mahendra master's shrill voice broke the pin-drop silence in the room.

Sanatan let out a sigh of relief at this. Looking at Prashanta, he now asked, 'Will you say something?'

Prashanta replied hesitantly, 'Is . . . is Atanu's story really *that* good?'

The tone of the teacher this time was devoid of anger or criticism. It now reflected a desire to discuss everything with an open mind. A gentle smile spread across Headmaster Santan's face. His work had become easy now. He glanced curiously at Anubhav; Anubhav was smiling too.

'I think Atanu wrote it really well,' Anubhav replied. 'The students were asked to write a story in their own language. I can easily infer that most of the students memorized the story from their textbooks and wrote it down verbatim. We tend to call things "well written" when someone memorizes a story and writes it down as it is, complete with the exact period, comma, semicolon and hyphen. But can we really call that "written in their own language"? Because, in reality, aren't they writing another person's story in that person's language? Where is the originality there? Where is the creativity in such a pursuit? Atanu was an exception in that regard. He wrote the story after interpreting and understanding it, in his own language. You will find that in Axomiya literature, some stories written in the regional dialect are highly appreciated by literary critics. Perhaps you already know that the renowned author Saurav Kumar Chaliha had written a short story by the name "Hahichampa". Saurav Chaliha wrote it in a regional Axomiya dialect. And this short story is considered one of the best short stories in Axomiya literature.' Pausing for a brief while, Anubhav said, 'Our little Atanu has tried something which only a seasoned author is capable of.'

Suddenly, a murmur that seemed to be one of appreciation filled the entire room, which gave Anubhav the courage to carry on, 'You know, I think our education system doesn't give importance to creativity. Students are not encouraged to think originally or innovatively. The intellectual development of students nurtured under such a system is not proper. I feel that some really extraordinary students also could not develop to their full potential at times because of this flawed system. Maybe, that's why, our people do not make it to the list of highly talented people in the world.'

'Hmm . . . I often mull over this matter. What is it that we lack when compared to other nations?' remarked Jilmil, a smart young teacher, sparking off a debate.

'We don't lack talent for sure,' replied Anubhav. 'But that talent doesn't get the conducive environment to develop fully owing to a variety of reasons. I think our curriculum, our pedagogy is to be blamed. There are anomalies in our examination system. Moreover, our entire education system is centred around examinations. Be it students, teachers or parents, we are occupied all the time with marks or percentages, which are considered the true parameters of measuring success and knowledge in the students.'

Gradually, the teachers who were silent all this time started to share their opinions as well. Jogesh sir now cut into the conversation. 'This year, the cut-off marks of a college under Delhi University reached 100 per cent! Imagine that.'

'Ah yes,' Chandan sighed. 'This mindless rat race breeds terrible tragedies . . . like my niece who committed suicide. She couldn't manage to get a seat at Delhi University despite scoring 97 per cent.'

'Well, it's so sad because in the BA final exam last year, 465 students secured first class from our university,' quipped Arunima.

'But what's the point? There is no value of these first classes!' exclaimed Debasish.

On seeing every teacher participate in the discussion, Anubhav felt gratified.

'What really happens is that the same questions are repeated in the exams year after year. If one peruses a few years' question papers, one can easily guess what questions are likely to be set in the exam,' explained Anubhav. 'Therefore, even if one studies mechanically without thinking or understanding anything, one can score good marks. This flawed examination system doesn't encourage students to develop original ideas or innovative thinking. If the questions in exams are set to test the original ideas and the creativity of the students, then the cut-off score cannot reach 100 per cent, nor will the number of students securing first class be exorbitantly high. Who knows, children will stop taking their precious lives even after securing 90 per cent and people will not mock the ones who are not able to secure high marks. I feel this will help ensure the education system nurtures talent and creativity over rote learning.'

'Then why don't the boards or the universities take steps to reform the examination system or the question papers?' asked Prashanta, who finally decided to participate in the discussion. To make him comfortable, no one reacted any differently.

'All of us want our students to get more and more marks.' It was the headmaster who answered. 'The feeling is that more marks will attract more students to their board or university. Students can opt for ICSE, CBSE and SEBA in Assam and other respective state boards in other states of India. They have options, and sadly, this has fuelled a competition as to which board or university can award more marks.'

'Exactly, sir!' exclaimed Anubhav. 'It's time to strictly regulate this examination system in a centralized way somewhere. And it is necessary that the marks awarded to students be normalized before college and university admissions take place. This step is essential as it will prevent any board or university to unnecessarily award more marks to their students, thereby giving them undue advantage. Otherwise, you will get to see that thousands of students of a particular board have scored 99 per cent marks while the topper of another board only scores 85 per cent marks. It is highly unlikely that all the good students are under one board while only the below average students are there in the other.'

'Yes, you're right,' nodded Gargi. 'Actually, if our examination system is reformed, lots of flaws in the system will get fixed automatically.'

'If our education system is fraught with so many shortcomings, what will be our responsibilities as simple schoolteachers? In this giant wheel of our education system, we are but minor cogs. What else can we do?' Headmaster Sanatan asked everybody with a heavy heart.

'It is a very complex question, sir,' Anubhav said. 'Still, I believe we should at least try to remain consistent in our efforts to educate the students in a proper way. We should promote original and creative ideas. We should teach them to analyse things logically. We should inspire them to develop independent and innovative ideas. We cannot simply wash our hands off by saying that the entire education system is rotten. It will lead to more problems and a lack of accountability. We, the teachers ourselves, will become the culprits then.'

After a long discussion, Sanatan proceeded to wind up the talk. It was already late in the evening. 'Our debates have taken us a long way. Yet, these are issues which need serious thought and attention. Anyway, let's come to the issue at hand now. Anubhav spoke about a lot of things today in his defence. I would like to hear your opinion now, Prashanta. Do you still have any grievance or anger against Anubhav?'

'Sir, I will think over the matter.' Prashanta winded up the issue immediately.

'Okay, think about it. Let me know what you wish to do.'

Just before concluding, Sanatan said abruptly, as if he had just recalled something, 'Mahendra hasn't returned yet. Where has he gone? Anubhav, please go and check outside.'

Anubhav came out to the veranda; however, Mahendra master was not there. He looked in every direction. Finally, he could spot him near the gate, standing under the bakul tree. Alone. It was darker under the tree canopy. But even now, it was beautiful. It added elegance to the school campus.

'Sir!' said Anubhav, reaching the gate.

'Oh, Anubhav! It's you.'

'Sir,' said Anubhav, standing next to the mathematics teacher, 'Why are you standing here? That too, all alone?'

'I am observing this bakul tree.'

'Hmm . . . yes, it's a beautiful tree.'

'Yes, quite wonderful.' Mahendra paused briefly. 'The idiot loved this tree a lot.'

'The idiot?' asked Anubhav, surprised.

'Ashim.'

19

As soon as Anubhav arrived at the school the following day, Headmaster Sanatan took him aside urgently.

'You have to teach mathematics to class X.'

Anubhav jumped! But it was Mahendra sir's class and subject! It would not be proper for him to take over like this, he thought. Plus, Mahendra sir was a teacher of renown and experience. Anubhav protested vehemently. 'No sir, I cannot do that. This year is very important for the students of class X.'

'Anubhav, please don't say no.'

'But Mahendra sir is a very good teacher!'

'Definitely! And it was Mahendra who asked me to assign the class to you.'

Anubhav was dumbfounded. He had no clue what was happening. But he knew that, for some reason, Mahendra had taken a liking to him and seemed to have great faith in his abilities. Anubhav too was fascinated by this strict disciplinarian with a hoarse voice, who was now in his late fifties. Anubhav could also judge that Mahendra had no malice in his mind and that inside his tough exterior, was a soft heart. He was reminded of a stream of pristine water gushing over hard rocks.

'And this is also Mahendra's earnest wish that you take this on,' saying these words, the headmaster left without waiting for Anubhav's reply.

*

On finding Anubhav alone during the lunch break, Mahendra master walked upto him. 'Has the headmaster spoken to you?'

'Yes, he has, but, sir . . .'

'Don't delay it, Anubhav. Take it on. Start teaching from tomorrow. I will take their last class today,' he said, interrupting Anubhav midway.

Mahendra got up and walked towards the door. On his way, he picked up a few bits of chalk and a duster and went out of the common room.

Is this seriously Mahendra sir's last class for class X? Anubhav wondered as he kept staring at the direction of the maths teacher's departure.

20

Mahendra master had just finished taking his last lesson for class X. He was now preparing to bid farewell to his students. He observed the faces of each student intently. Overcome with emotion, he tried to process the thought that he would not teach them anymore. It would be a different matter to teach them occasionally in the absence of Anubhav, but yes nothing would be the same again.

Mahendra master started to feel a little sad gazing at the children's faces. Although he scolded them often, he also felt at peace with himself whenever he saw them in front of his eyes. Towards the end of each year, while teaching the students of class X, he always felt a kind of unexplainable sadness in his heart as he knew that the kids would leave the school forever. After that, he would chance upon them sometime, somewhere. And when he did meet an old student, he would feel as if he had met someone very close to him and he would be thrilled, overwhelmed with joy. However, the student would usually remain distant and wouldn't want to come closer to their old teacher. When this happened, Mahendra master would feel pained. And this happened often.

This year, he had to part with the students only three months after the year had begun. Mahendra master readied himself to convey this information to the students, 'Okay, so tell me, children, how do you find your new teacher?'

Everyone shouted in unison, 'Good! Very good!'

Mahendra chuckled. *Anubhav has already won over their hearts*, he thought.

'Ah! So, Anubhav is good! Very good, but what about me, you idiots? Am I that bad?'

Upon hearing Mahendra sir's words, the students started to snigger and laugh too. But soon, their smiles disappeared. Mustering a little courage, a student called Gitali offered, 'You are also very good, sir!'

'Okay, okay, leave it. You won't say I'm horrid to my face, now, will you?' he laughed.

Nirmal, who was also in the class, sensed a tinge of sorrow in his teacher's voice. Mahendra sir's angry and terrifying persona had surely left an indelible imprint on everyone's minds. However, Nirmal recalled something that had taken place some days ago, something that showed another facet of Mahendra sir's personality. Something so unimaginable and well concealed that Nirmal couldn't believe his eyes.

Three months ago, in this very same classroom, everyone had fallen absolutely silent. There had been no sound from anyone's mouth. Nobody had budged, even a little, from their places. It had been as if the students had even forgotten to breathe. It was the day when Mahendra sir had beaten Ashim till he drew blood. Sitting right next to Ashim and watching the horror from close quarters, Nirmal had become immensely disappointed and disgusted with his teacher.

As Ashim had run away from the class, with his blood trailing behind him, Nirmal had looked towards the direction in which his friend had departed. He was hypnotized by the trail of red blood that dotted the floor. Following the blood, Nirmal's eyes had stopped at the doorway of the classroom. He was dumbstruck, for he could see that Mahendra sir was standing at the doorway. In his hands were a bottle of antiseptic and a roll of cotton. Casting a glance across the room, he asked Nirmal, 'Where has that idiot gone?'

Ashim had not witnessed that scene. And Nirmal had never told him about it either, as he didn't want to hurt Ashim any further.

Following that day, on several occasions, Mahendra master had enquired about Ashim and his whereabouts.

'How is that idiot?'

With deep anguish in his heart, Nirmal answered every time, 'I don't know, sir.'

*

'So, from tomorrow onwards, the new teacher will teach you maths . . .' Mahendra master stopped midway, his throat heavily choked. Swallowing hard, he said, 'This is my last class with you. Study well, you idiots.'

The class was still, confused. Silent.

Taking the chalk and the duster, Mahendra sir proceeded towards the doorway. Stopping for a moment, he turned around and looking towards Nirmal, he asked, 'Why does your idiot friend enjoy getting drenched in the rain?'

Failing to comprehend anything, Nirmal looked up, confused.

'I am talking about Ashim,' clarified Mahendra master but without waiting for Nirmal's reply, he left the room in a hurry, rapidly walking away.

21

The proposal of teaching class X made Anubhav both happy and uneasy at the same time. Firstly, he was overwhelmed by the trust that two experienced senior teachers of the school had shown him. But at the same time, he felt very uneasy having to replace a renowned teacher like Mahendra master. However, the request had come from a place of affection and from two people who were around his father's age. The situation dictated that Anubhav's willingness or unwillingness had very little significance.

Wrapped up in these thoughts, Anubhav went out of the school gate and stepped onto the main road. As he moved a couple of yards, he heard someone calling him from behind, 'Hey, wait for me!'

Anubhav turned around to see Jilmil, the young female faculty member. She smiled a little.

'I can go to my house via the road that leads to your rented house. So, let's walk together?' she asked. 'I'll just have to go a little farther but that's not a problem. Let's go?' offered Jilmil.

Anubhav nodded but felt a little uncomfortable. Jilmil had chosen to take the longer route just for his company, and he didn't know what to make of it.

On the way, Jilmil started to chat, 'I think you can see for yourself that the people in this village are not very well off. For some parents, sending their children to school is nothing but a waste of time and money. That's why several children drop out of school midway. Many kids don't even enrol in college after passing the matriculation examination. Poor souls, they take up odd jobs to help their parents earn a living,' added Jilmil, sighing. 'It all contributes. The condition of the village is also not good. I mean, you have seen the state of the roads. Ours is the only high school in the area, and it is in a dilapidated state. Leave aside lights, fans, etc., even the blackboards are not in good condition! And let's not even talk about the state of the washrooms! They are just makeshift restrooms made of areca leaves and jute stalks. Do you know, because of this, many girls don't even enrol? The few who do enrol, drop out after a year or two. When I see the expensive schools in towns, I feel pity for our students. You know, with the yearly fees of just one child who goes to such a school, we can build five or more proper washrooms here.'

'You think very deeply,' murmured Anubhav, impressed.

Jilmil shrugged. 'I don't *think*. I used to earlier. But now, I have given up thinking. What's the point, anyway?

Governments come, governments go; people stand in queues to cast their votes. However, this village, this school, all remain the same. They get worse, not better.'

'Doesn't the local MLA do anything?'

Jilmil let out a sad smile. 'The local MLA does a thing or two. But things get old with time. The roads wear out, so does the school building. The little amount of work that the government does cannot drastically improve the condition overnight. Most of what they can do is repair work. And after all that addition and subtraction, the condition gets from bad to worse. However, the contractors and the middlemen, not to mention the ministers and the MLAs, get richer day by day. It's common knowledge that most of the money in a majority of these improvement schemes is misused.'

Anubhav nodded and added, 'And in spite of all these issues, people cast their votes to elect the same type of leaders again and again.'

'Yes,' she answered, walking briskly. 'I guess it is because we are also corrupt mentally.' She smiled. 'In the name of government schemes, our leaders have made provisions for us to eat two square meals a day, but there is no talk of jobs. Then, of course, the usual business of handing over people a couple of hundred rupees and a blanket before the elections as doles. This makes sure that all the eligible family members cast their votes in favour of that leader. People neither have earnings nor savings. So, whenever a family member falls seriously ill, they have to sell their farmland, which was their means of survival in the first place.' The two teachers walked for a long time immersed in their own thoughts.

'You know, if the government creates more jobs, it's not just the people who will benefit; but the country's economy will become stronger too,' said Anubhav after a while. 'There is a famous Chinese proverb: give a person a fish, he will eat for one day; teach him how to catch that fish, he will be able to eat fish for a lifetime.'

'Of course,' agreed Jilmil. 'But successive governments misappropriate public funds and buy the votes by baiting people with one or two fish every now and then. Quite evidently, they don't want people to start fishing. Because when people's thoughts become free from the worry of hunger, they will pose a threat to these cunning leaders. They want people to be dependent on them. I mean, how else will they be able to procure people's votes? They can only do so by enticing or blackmailing them.'

'You're right, Jilmil. Plus, the leaders don't do proper research, nor do they have a blueprint or serious thought about meaningful progress. For that matter, they don't have anything that is needed to prepare genuinely effective welfare schemes.'

'Sadly, knowledgeable people with intellectual capacity don't enter politics,' added Jilmil.

The two now walked on the dusty main road that dipped in places where it had worn out. Little kids ran behind a tyre, hitting it with a twig and giggling merrily. The two teachers observed the passers-by for a while.

'People with integrity also don't have black money,' remarked Anubhav after some time. 'At least, they don't have enough to win an election. The other day, I saw on the news that, on an average, there are about 2200 polling stations in a parliamentary constituency. On the day of the election, three or four youngsters from each of the political parties sit outside each of the polling stations and document the voters' serial numbers and attendance. Now, if these people are given even Rs 500 daily, then, the total cost, multiplying the 2200 stations by 500, would amount to Rs 11 lakhs!'

Jilmil agreed. 'So true. In addition to this, there are other expenditures—the election offices opened across the constituencies—these are open for months till the election, not to mention the petrol and diesel for the hundreds of bikes and cars that are used for campaigning, and myriad other expenses.'

'All this is minus the money spent on liquor and blankets, used as bribes. Imagine, this is not even by one political party, but by many! So, yes, a person who doesn't have money in crores cannot even think of winning an election. I mean, who will participate to merely lose? It's the dishonest and cunning leaders with money who generally keep on winning elections. Whatever they do, they do for self-gain and not for the welfare of the public. If they spend Rs 1 crore in an election, they try to embezzle Rs 10 crores in the next five years. They make up for what they've spent. Election has now become a business,' saying this, Anubhav took a deep breath.

Jilmil sighed. 'We have only ourselves to blame. Till we start casting our votes with responsibility and without being lured by anyone, these people will keep winning.'

'Right,' said Anubhav. 'We need to create an atmosphere where people with integrity can thrive. We ordinary citizens have only one weapon against these cunning politicians—our right to vote. We have to exercise this right with utmost honesty.'

They walked some distance silently, absorbed in these thoughts. Suddenly, a motorbike zoomed past them, throwing up clouds of dust before disappearing at the bend in the road.

Jilmil, who had jumped to the side, looked in the direction of the disappearing biker angrily, 'Now, look at that buffoon! The way the number of bikes is increasing in the village!' she grumbled. 'You know a few here have even bought four-wheelers! People who don't even have proper toilets in their house carry smartphones in their hands. The tendency to show off has increased so much. It's all about what glitters on the outside. Look at Bihu and Durga Puja festivities; the fancy display and fanfare on the cultural nights is just next level! Everything is gold on the outside, hollow from the inside. Gambling and drinking—these rowdy boys constantly use filthy and obscene language—they show off their bikes with dangerous stunts and show no respect for public safety!'

'You feel quite deeply for your village!' remarked Anubhav, observing Jilmil.

'No, I don't. I've told you already. I *used to* think earlier. Now, I don't. I've given up. I am doing my job and getting paid for that. That's it. I'm now eating, sleeping and living happily. That's all.'

After a brief pause, they walked on. Just as the sun was setting, Jilmil turned to Anubhav and said, 'You know, at first sight, the village appears . . . how you say it, in a festive mood. Everything is a facade, though. If you look closely, you'll not see a single tangible dream in anyone's eyes. Do you know what that is like?' she asked softly.

Anubhav looked at her intently, his breath getting heavy. He shook his head.

'There was once a young man in our village. He was very cheerful and fun-loving. He was always at the forefront—be it dance, drama, music, Bihu celebrations, Puja, or anyone's wedding ceremony. Wherever he was present, he would create a festive atmosphere around himself. But to everyone's utter shock, he committed suicide one night. Perhaps he had been suffering from acute depression, who knows?'

Both became silent for a while. Anubhav understood that Jilmil wanted to let off steam and share the thoughts that she'd been bottling up inside of her for a long time. He looked at her encouragingly.

'The condition of our village is like that boy. This village celebrates so many festivals throughout the year and seems to be perpetually immersed in festive spirits, but, in reality, it is actually suffering from acute depression. Or what do you call it? Mass depression.'

'Mass depression?' asked Anubhav, shocked.

'Yes, mass depression,' she shrugged. 'I am also a part of that depression. I have become a machine. I gave up thinking about all these things. But . . .' All of a sudden, Jilmil stopped speaking.

Anubhav looked at her anxiously.

'But after meeting you, I feel like thinking about all those things again.' Anubhav was taken aback. Surprised by this, he looked toward his colleague and locked eyes with her. In those glittering discs, she saw a thousand dreams crammed in.

When she noticed Anubhav looking at her in this manner, Jilmil let out a loud, spontaneous laughter.

22

Anubhav woke up to the phone ringing loudly. In the darkness, he extended his hand outside the mosquito net and picked up the phone.

'Hello, Anubhav. It's me. I just finished reading Saurav Kumar Chaliha's "Hahichampa". I read it twice, actually. And my! What an excellent piece of writing! I liked it very much. I hope you don't mind me calling you now . . . I felt like conveying my feelings to you immediately after reading it . . . I know it's midnight . . . very late . . . And do you know one thing, Anubhav? Our Atanu wrote the story well. I mean very well. Hello! Hello! Are you listening? Anubhav? Hello? Have you fallen asleep? Why aren't you saying anything?'

This was the problem with Anubhav. His eyes tended to well up quickly.

After listening to Prashanta's midnight monologue, Anubhav once again felt a sense of reassurance. When one approached people with honesty and sincerity, they responded with the same sincerity and candour as well.

The incident, which had previously widened the gap between him and his colleagues, had, in fact, brought them closer.

23

As Anubhav was taking attendance, he stopped at the last roll number. Ashim! *This boy has been absent for the last three months,* he thought. After closing the attendance register, he asked the children, 'Okay, what has happened to this boy named Ashim? He has not come to school for a long, long time.'

Nirmal saw a glimmer of hope at the question posed by his new maths teacher. He stood up. 'Sir, he has dropped out of school.'

Anubhav remained silent for a few seconds. He wanted to say something but decided against it. 'Meet me after school hours, Nirmal,' is all he said, gesturing for the boy to sit.

The class had fallen silent, and everyone seemed to be awaiting instructions from the new teacher.

'I will teach you mathematics from today. We've already been introduced by the headmaster. I have my own method of teaching. And I will not teach you anything from the textbook today. Today, I want to chat with you and tell you something which I think is very important. So, let's start, shall we? Now, who in this class loves mathematics?'

Anubhav saw that only three boys raised their hands. Anubhav was not at all surprised by this. He said with a smile, 'Rest of you don't love mathematics, then? So, you must find it difficult?'

'No . . . yes . . . sir. We find mathematics difficult, which is why we don't like it.' It was Simanta who had answered.

Boys like Simanta had never had the opportunity of speaking to their teacher face-to-face. So, it was quite evident that Simanta was breathless as he spoke. It was because of Anubhav sir's frank question that he could even muster the courage to do so.

Looking at the boy, Anubhav replied, 'Oh, is it so? But when you dislike something, there has to be a reason behind it. Will you start disliking me, too, if I teach you the subject you hate?'

Everybody laughed as they shouted, 'No, sir! No, sir!' Indeed, they didn't dislike Anubhav. Simanta, Nirmal and the other students were overwhelmed by the resonance of their own shout! Not just in mathematics class; they weren't allowed to speak freely at all in any class!

Taking a long, deep breath and putting one of his hands on his chest dramatically, Anubhav declared, 'Oh, thank god, I'm saved!'

On seeing the teacher's act, everyone laughed.

Looking at Simanta, Anubhav now said, 'Since you find maths difficult, you dislike it. Thereafter, maths becomes more difficult for you, doesn't it? And the more difficult you find maths, the more you start disliking it, isn't it? It's a vicious cycle.'

Simanta nodded his head in agreement. He was amazed! He wondered how this new teacher could know what was going on in his mind! It was true; the more Simanta disliked maths, the less time he devoted to it. But his parents were not aware of this habit of his, as he would regularly lie to them. The sad fact remained that as he moved up to higher classes, the more he found maths excruciatingly difficult and unappealing.

Releasing a deep sigh, Anubhav continued, 'What to do? What to do . . . you know, children, there is more to this poor guy called "maths". You see, the more you dislike him, the more *he* will become intimidating, disobedient and even rowdy! Because he will feel bad that you are rejecting him. But the moment you start showing him affection, he will become a likeable and an obedient student.'

Could it be like that? For the first time, Simanta and his classmates felt pity for maths. So much pity! Focusing on their hearing like alert rabbits, they started absorbing every word spoken by their new teacher.

'You know Mahatma Gandhi was in a similar condition as you all. In his autobiography, *My Experiments with Truth,* he wrote about this. You see, Gandhi found geometry very difficult. But one day, while studying a theorem, he realized that a subject where logic was used couldn't be that difficult for him. Since the moment of that realization, Gandhi wrote, the subject became easy for him.'

Anubhav paused to observe the kids; they were all listening intently.

'Do you know what usually happens in classes?' he asked them. 'You just memorize the formulae and, later, looking at a maths problem solved by your teacher, you solve five other similar problems. That's what you call "practising maths". You never try to "think" on your own. Apply yourself. Perhaps we teachers also don't give you that opportunity,' he said sadly. 'As a result, even after knowing all the formulae, whenever you come across a new type of problem—that has not been solved for you by your teacher before—you just keep sitting there, twirling the pen. You can't even proceed a little on your own. It's like someone who is thrown into the pool, but doesn't know how to swim, isn't it?'

This time, no one made a single sound. In fact, everyone was holding their breath. They felt as if even a minor sound would shatter the atmosphere of the wonderful things they were listening to. So, they all just nodded silently—yes, they too had that feeling.

'All these issues combined don't help nurture the habit of thinking and of analysing something logically in you students. And this is what makes you weak in maths. This is why, when a new or a complicated problem is set in an exam, you cannot solve it. As a result, you lose marks in the exams. But that is a minor loss. Students become adults who don't try to think logically or don't want to think for themselves. And when they leave school and go out into society, this causes damage to the society, albeit invisibly. Someone who has not learnt to think deeply would then roam the streets, bullying others. They could plant a bomb somewhere or even take someone's life. If people try to think on their own and think deeply, half the problems plaguing society will vanish automatically, I feel. All these issues are also related to education. The goal of education is not just to get good marks in exams and to secure a good job. It's more than that.'

Anubhav paused and scanned the faces of his students. He wondered whether what he was telling them was going over their heads. Was it tough for the students of class X to comprehend? As he looked at the faces of the students, he felt a kind of affection for them. They were listening to him intently, even though they might not have understood everything. *There is no harm in not understanding everything*, thought Anubhav. After all, it is only when one's eyes really notice something, there arises an intrinsic desire to *see* and know more about it. That was why Anubhav decided to tell the students a few more things.

'You know, children, perhaps we put more stress on your ability to memorize. For example, think about the multiplication table. I think it is more than sufficient to know the multiplication tables of 2, 3, 4, 5, 6, 7, 8 and 9. There is nothing much to memorize in the multiplication table of 5. The other seven multiplication tables are also not that difficult to remember. But we ask you to memorize twenty multiplication tables from 1 to 20. Earlier, when students failed to memorize and recall multiplication tables, teachers would use corporal punishment.' He smiled. 'You know, when I was in school like you and had once failed to memorize the required multiplication tables, I stopped going to school for fear of being beaten by my teacher! I didn't go to school for many, many days, in fact. Then, finally, one day, my father went to my school and met with my teacher. It was only after my teacher assured my father that he would never beat me again that I rejoined classes. And now, as you can see, I have become a teacher of mathematics myself! If my father had not done what he did, my education would have stopped at class II or III itself.'

A murmur rippled through the entire classroom. It seemed like the new teacher was just like them! Such a pleasant surprise! Everyone in class now started to sympathize and feel a familiarity towards Anubhav. They felt close to him! Hadn't they too put in so much hard work to memorize the multiplication tables? Many among them had been scolded so many times, too! Just as Anubhav sir had mentioned, they too had received lashes. Two of their classmates had even dropped out of school out of fear of getting caned every day.

They could hear Anubhav sir speaking again, 'If you ask me now, "Sir, tell us 19 x 7 is equal to what?" I will not be able to answer it instantly. Maybe, Nirmal could answer it before me. But, even if I'm a few seconds late, I'll give the answer. And I will give the answer correctly. The product 20 x 7 is easy to calculate. 2 x 7 = 14. Therefore, 20 x 7 = 140. But I need the product of 19 x 7, that is, 19 times 7, not

20 times 7. One 7 less. Therefore, I will subtract one 7 from 140. Therefore, the product of 19 x 7 is 133. I will definitely need a few seconds more to calculate this. But, there is no irksome feeling of having to memorize the multiplication table of 19 and I would arrive at the answer logically on my own.

'Again, assume that you've gone to a vegetable market. And that you've bought 22 kilograms of a particular vegetable at a rate of Rs 17 per kilogram. How much do you need to pay the vendor? Before giving money to the man, you might be thinking and calculating in your head, just when the vegetable vendor will say out loud, "Rs 374". Now, how did he calculate that so quickly? Firstly, he calculated the price of 20 kilograms of vegetables, which is Rs 340. Since you've bought 22 kilograms, he will add the price of 2 kilograms, that is, Rs 34 to the price of 20 kilograms. The vegetable vendor and I have done the same thing to arrive at the answer. Now look here. This is what the vegetable vendor has done—'

Taking a piece of chalk pencil, Anubhav started writing on the blackboard:

$$22 \times 17 = (20 + 2) \times 17$$
$$= 20 \times 17 + 2 \times 17 \quad (??)$$
$$= 2 \times 17 \times 10 + 2 \times 17$$
$$= 34 \times 10 + 34$$
$$= 340 + 34$$
$$= 374$$

'And see what I have done—' So saying, Anubhav sir resumed writing on the board.

$$19 \times 7 \quad = (20 - 1) \times 7$$
$$= 20 \times 7 - 1 \times 7 \quad (??)$$
$$= 2 \times 7 \times 10 - 7$$
$$= 140 - 7$$
$$= 133$$

The students noticed that Anubhav sir had put two question marks at two places. Looking towards them, he now asked them, 'I've put two question marks at two places. Can you tell me which law of mathematics is applied there?'

There was no response from anyone. Anubhav waited for a while before asking them again, 'Think it over a little.'

Anubhav waited again. Still, there was no reply.

'Have you heard about distributive laws?'

This time, a number of students shouted together. They said in one breath:

$$a(b + c) = ab + ac$$
and $\quad (a + b)c = ac + bc.$

Anubhav chuckled.

'Yes!' he laughed. 'Yes! The first one is left distributive law, and the second one is right distributive law. Actually, the vegetable vendor and I have done the calculations orally, applying distributive law. Many vegetable vendors might not have even heard about the name of distributive laws, but they have applied logic and used critical thinking.'

The students observed that, while explaining this, the new teacher had not made fun of the vegetable vendors. Rather, he praised them.

Anubhav then explained to them how he and the vendor had applied the distributive laws.

He now put three dots on the blackboard:

A
.

B .

. C

The students stared at the board with full attention. They had discovered a new flavour in the maths class today. Anubhav told them, 'Assume that A, B and C are three different places. And you are supposed to go from A to C. Which route will you take? Will you go along the AC route or will you first take the AB route and then the BC route?'

Anubhav completed the picture:

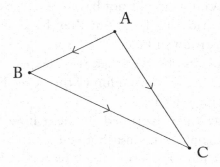

All the students shouted in unison, 'AC route, sir!'

'Yes. Very good. AC route. If both the routes are either equally good or equally bad, you will take the AC route. But tell me, why?'

A mischievous boy called Ananda got up. 'It is a short cut, that's why!'

Anubhav smiled. 'Yes, short cut. Even a person with no formal education will arrive at this conclusion. Actually, a beautiful theorem of geometry is at play here. Can anyone tell me which one?'

Everyone remained silent. Anubhav gave them a cue. 'ABC—what is it?'

This time, several students shouted, 'Triangle!'

Without giving them the answer, Anubhav asked them again, 'Can you tell me now which theorem is being used here?'

'The sum of the lengths of any two sides of a triangle is greater than the length of the third side,' Nirmal said spiritedly.

'Yes, you are correct.' As he said this, Anubhav noticed that Nirmal's eyes were shinning in delight—the excitement and delight of *discovering* something.

'Just see how we are using this triangle theorem or the distributive law in our daily lives without being aware of them!' he said.

Anubhav observed the students intently. A wave of happiness seemed to reflect on their faces.

'I have already told you that we stress more on memorizing. Look at literature. In the exams of lower classes, students are asked to write down the first eight lines of any poem from their memory. Even if you don't like that poem, you *have to* commit it to memory. If you don't, you lose marks in exams. Tell me, what is the need for memorizing? Understanding the poem is the more important thing. First, try to understand the poem and, if you can, write one yourself. What is the need for memorizing? If you love a particular poem, and if that poem stays in your memory because of repeated reading, that's quite all right. The same is the case with mathematical formulae. When you understand formulae, they stay in your memory automatically. If you keep on memorizing the formulae without understanding them, the higher you climb the academic ladder, the heavier the load of the formulae will be, which will make your thoughts go awry. Just as a computer hangs or freezes when too many files are saved in it, you will not be able to process information nor recollect it as and when you need it. By the way, tell me, are you feeling bored?'

'No, sir!' the students responded immediately.

'Great! Then listen to this story. Once, a person asked Albert Einstein about a minor matter related to physics. Einstein politely informed him that he had no knowledge about the matter. The person was surprised and said to Einstein, "You are such a great scientist, and yet you don't know about this?" Do you know what Einstein said in his response? He said, "I don't carry information in my mind that is readily available in books."'

'But, sir, we have to commit certain things to memory for exams!' interjected Ananda.

Anubhav nodded. 'Definitely, you have to. But it should be as little as possible. Your emphasis should be on *understanding* the concepts. Only then will you be able to enjoy your studies, irrespective of the subject. If you are able to solve a new type of mathematical problem, which nobody taught you before, then you will find joy or should find joy there. Just like the joy of creating a new thing. I am telling you about all these things in my very first class. When you come to my class, attend it with this frame of mind. I'll attempt to simplify the concepts in a way that makes it easier for you to understand. But don't expect that I will be able to make each and every concept of mathematics as easy as ABC. I will try to explain to you the various concepts of mathematics without oversimplifying the main principles. Even if you find certain concepts difficult, try to enjoy their beauty. It is not proper to teach something incorrectly or to teach something disregarding the actual things, just to make the topic simple. Assume that you are riding a bicycle on a zigzag road. If you try riding your bicycle in a linear direction, disregarding the fact that you are on a zigzag road, won't you ultimately tumble into a roadside ditch? Take another example. Consider a tree whose branches are shooting off in different directions. In order to make that tree straight, if you cut off the branches of that tree, the tree might appear all spruced up and straight, but will that tree retain its beauty and original form?'

As the class absorbed this perspective, Anubhav paused for a while.

'Now, I understand that many of you might not study mathematics as a subject in the future. But don't ignore mathematics because of that. In our society, the number of people who can think logically are far less in number. Mathematics helps us think logically. If a society is to run properly, subjects like mathematics and sciences should not just remain subjects taught in schools and colleges. They should be part of life. Therefore, when you study, don't simply think of doing well in exams. Think about the big picture too. You should develop this kind of thinking starting now. Remember one thing— it's very easy to be a patriot by burning firecrackers when India wins against Pakistan in a cricket match. However, someone who does everything keeping in mind the aforesaid things is a patriot in the true sense.'

It was time for the school bell to ring and for the class to be over. Anubhav got ready to wind up the class. 'Now, I will give you three questions. You can consult any book you want. You can even discuss amongst yourselves. I will give you seven days' time to solve them. Now take down these three questions:

'First question: Think about nine-digit numbers where each of the digits from 1 to 9 is used once and only once to form the number. For example, 827543619 is one such number. There are a lot of numbers like this. Mind it—I am saying it again—whatever number you take, each digit should appear there once and only once. Now my question is how many of these will be prime numbers?

'Second question: Give an example of twenty consecutive composite numbers.

'Third question: You are given a circle. You have to find the centre of the circle using only a pencil and set square from your geometry box.' Saying this, he took a geometry box from a student and showed them the set square.

'If you are able to get answers to these three questions, it will be very good. But if you fail to get the answers, don't get disheartened. Just try to work on them with all sincerity. Do your best. You can learn many things when you try sincerely.' Having finished his class, Anubhav went out of the classroom.

That day, the hearts of Nirmal and his classmates were filled with an inexplicable joy. They started discussing the questions excitedly the moment their teacher left the room. One of them drew a circle and tried to find its centre by taking out the set square. They were unsure where to begin. Till now, they had never come across such types of questions! Though the problems appeared somewhat weird to them, but their minds repeatedly turned towards them like magnets.

On the other hand, Nirmal had been thinking about Ashim throughout the class. Now listening to his classmates' attempts and their excitement, the recollections increased manifold. Nirmal felt an intense urge to share the questions with Ashim. Just as when you get a piece of good news and you instantly want to share it with your loved ones as soon as possible! And Nirmal couldn't help but notice that Anubhav sir had asked him about Ashim. Through this new teacher, Nirmal could see a faint ray of hope.

24

After the school was over and as discussed in class, Nirmal walked to the teacher's common room. On seeing the boy, Anubhav came out of the common room. The other students had already left for home, and the teachers had also started to leave.

Anubhav took Nirmal aside. 'Okay. Now tell me why Ashim has dropped out of school.'

'There are a lot of reasons, sir!' said Nirmal, before pausing for a while. He took a deep breath and then slowly started to speak. He spoke about a lot of things—things he knew, things he saw and things he thought about, about the condition of Ashim's family, about Ashim's father and his alcohol addiction, about Ashim's worsening academic life, about teachers' growing dissatisfaction with him, about Nirmal's own efforts to bring Ashim back to school, about Ashim's return to school, about Mahendra sir's ill-treatment of him and the corporal punishment meted out to him, about Ashim's leaving school thereafter for good, about the incident in which the villagers had punished and humiliated Ashim's father and about Ashim's decision and his hard labour in the quarry. Nirmal poured his heart out. At the end, he added, 'You have to bring him back, sir. Only you can do this. Please.'

Anubhav looked affectionately at Nirmal and said, 'I will go to Ashim's house tomorrow with you.'

Hearing these words, Nirmal's mind danced with joy. Seeing hope for Ashim's return to school, his happiness knew no bounds! With gratitude in his eyes, Nirmal said, 'That would be very nice of you, sir. But we will be able to meet Ashim only if we go to his house after 6 p.m.'

'Okay, no problem. At 6 p.m., I will pick you up from your house. Now, go home.'

Nirmal got ready to leave. Just after taking a step forward, he stopped. 'Sir, I want to say something to you. I am not sure whether we will be able to solve the three problems you gave us today in class. But, I believe, Ashim can solve these three problems. You see, sir, he is amazingly sharp when it comes to mathematics. Everyone here knew that he was intelligent. But I feel nobody could fathom how brilliant he is in mathematics. Even he himself isn't fully aware of his abilities.'

'But you are aware!' said Anubhav smiling.

Nirmal nodded. 'I have a sense of his abilities. But I don't have the capacity to gauge his intelligence. You, on the other hand, can assess him. I think you will feel very happy when you meet him. And he—he will be very happy too to meet you, I am sure.'

This boy has a heart of gold. Unlike some other toppers, he is not selfish, thought Anubhav as he watched Nirmal leave.

25

Nirmal felt very happy. His mind was filled with a lot of hope. He was finding it hard to contain his happiness and the hope bubbling inside his heart. He felt an intense urge to share all these things with Ashim. Therefore, without going home directly from school, he headed straightaway to the quarry at the foot of the hill.

He saw that Ashim and his companions were hard at work, breaking stones in the quarry. They were all surprised to see Nirmal walking towards them with his school bag.

'You too have dropped out of school then and have come to breakdown stones here, Mr Jewel No. 2?' Ramen attacked Nirmal, sniggering.

Hearing the tone of Ramen's voice, Nirmal became nervous. Nirmal's world was far removed from this. Ramen used to ridicule Ashim horribly, but, over time, he began to tolerate him. This was partly because Ashim too had dropped out of school as a result of Mahendra sir's beatings and verbal abuse. However, even now, at the slightest opportunity, the boy would not leave the chance to mock Ashim as 'the jewel'. It was quite clear that Ramen felt a kind of pleasure from bullying Ashim. On the other hand, the snide remarks would pinch Ashim and make him suffer silently.

'What happened, Jewel No. 2? Cat got your tongue?' Ramen started again.

Nirmal remained silent.

Suddenly, Ashim roared at him, 'If you say anything to Nirmal again, I will thrash your head with this hammer!' Raising his hammer, he stared down at Ramen in rage.

Ramen couldn't muster the courage to retaliate. He was shocked; he had ridiculed Ashim many times, but this was the first time that the boy had retaliated.

Ashim stood up. Throwing his hammer onto a heap of stones, he told Nirmal, 'Let's get out of here.'

The two boys moved away and sat on a flat bed of rock. On noticing Nirmal observing him with a look of surprise, Ashim asked, 'What happened?'

'Would you have really thrashed Ramen with that hammer?'

'I don't know,' Ashim replied curtly.

Nirmal remained silent.

'Are you afraid of me now?' asked Ashim. 'Will you not come to meet me in the future?'

'You've changed a lot.' Nirmal's voice was heavy.

'He teased you. He was picking on you—that's why I reacted that way,' Ashim tried to explain with much effort.

'If one starts thrashing someone's head over such trivial matters, then nobody will have a head without a crack, Ashim,' Nirmal said quietly.

'Don't worry, your head will remain intact,' Ashim shot back.

'There is no need for you to crack anybody's head here,' saying this Nirmal looked at Ashim squarely. 'You have to come back to school,' he said adamantly.

'What?' Ashim jumped to his feet. He took a few seconds to fully comprehend what Nirmal had just said, then with a view to making the matter light, said, 'If you say this again, I will thrash your head into pieces, too.'

'Do it,' said Nirmal gently.

Ashim didn't speak.

Nirmal spoke again, with force, 'You'll go to school or you'll have to thrash my head.'

'I am not going to school, nor am I thrashing your head,' Ashim added, sighing.

'Fine! Then, I'll break your head into pieces,' threatened Nirmal.

Ashim turned serious this time. He said without looking at Nirmal, 'You have come here to say this only?'

'Yes.'

'Why have you brought up this issue again, Nirmal?' Ashim uttered the words in deep anguish.

'Did I say anything after that day's incident?'

Ashim didn't reply.

'Things have changed at school,' Nirmal tried again.

Ashim turned his head in a different direction. Though he wasn't looking at his best friend, he was listening to him intently.

'Mahendra sir no longer teaches us maths.'

I don't have anything to do with that.

'A new teacher has come.'

Yes, Nirmal had shared the same information the other day as well.

'Our new teacher is very good. He loves us a lot.'

Hmm . . . Nirmal had mentioned this too. What do I have to do with any of that?

'He started teaching us maths from today.'

Good.

'He told us about a lot of things today.'

Very good.

'He has given us three maths questions to solve.'

Has he?

'Would you like to hear what the questions are?'

You can tell me if you want to. Anyway, you are continuously talking whether I am paying attention to you or not!

'A circle is given. With the help of a pencil and a set square from the geometry box, we have to find the centre of the circle.'

Set square, set square—oh yes!

'Are you listening to me?'

The circle's centre is to be found?

'The second question is . . .'

Diameter bisects a circle.

'Are you listening?'

Two diameters will intercept each other at the centre.

'What are you thinking?'

Ashim slid down from the rock. He stood on the road under the hill. Raising his head, he saw that Nirmal was still sitting at the top and looking down at him, surprised.

'Come down,' Ashim hollered.

Surprised, Nirmal slid down.

Taking a pebble, Ashim drew a circle on the ground. 'Look here—if we make the vertex of the right angle of the set square touch the circle, the two sides making the right angle of the set square will intercept the circle at two points. The line drawn by joining the two points will be the diameter of the circle.'

'Why?'

'The angle on a semi-circle is a right angle, isn't it?' Ashim reminded Nirmal.

'Yes . . . yes. And after that?'

'Draw another diameter just like that,' said Ashim, drawing.

'Okay, so . . .'

'So, the point at which both these diameters intercept each other is the centre!' Ashim said triumphantly.

Startled, Nirmal looked at Ashim. He noticed that his friend's eyes had started sparkling with excitement. And a beautiful smile had spread across his face. It had been an all too familiar sight just three years ago. Ashim had yet again easily solved a difficult maths problem which Nirmal had been mulling over, unable to solve. After he'd solved it, his face would light up just as it had today. The pleasure and excitement of solving a maths problem! It was the same today. In fact, today everyone in class had tried to work on the problem throughout the day. But no one was able to solve it!

On seeing Nirmal's surprised look, Ashim asked him, smiling, 'What happened?'

'What about the other two questions?' Concealing his amazement, Nirmal pretended to rebuke Ashim.

'I didn't hear the other two questions.'

'Idiot!' Nirmal rolled his eyes.

'Fine. Tell me again?'

Nirmal repeated the two questions. This time, Ashim heard him attentively. While climbing up the rock again, he said, 'Interesting questions. But I'll have to think. I can't answer right away.'

'Well. Tell me now, Ashim. What do you think of our new teacher?' asked Nirmal clambering up the rock behind him.

It seemed that at that very moment, everything changed. Darkness enveloped the light. It was as if Ashim had again fallen flat on the hard rock of reality. The maths problems had taken him back to his happier days. Nirmal noticed the smile on Ashim's face as well as the sparkle in his eyes were gone now.

'What are you thinking?' Nirmal asked Ashim.

'Nothing,' Ashim replied, concealing his feelings.

'You're thinking about something.'

'No!'

'Will you come back to school?'

It's been three months since I've left school.

'You have to rejoin!'

I won't return to school.

'You must go.'

I can't go. A lot has changed by now.

'Why don't you understand what I'm trying to say?'

Nirmal would never be able to understand my situation. The responsibilities of the entire household rest on my shoulders now.

'Why don't you say anything?'

What can I say? How much can I confide in Nirmal? Where do I begin? And where would it end?

'Our new teacher asked about you today.'

The words hit Ashim like a thunderclap! Dumbstruck, Ashim kept staring at Nirmal.

'He has asked me to take him to your house tomorrow.'

As if lightening had struck Ashim. His eyes widened out of fright and surprise.

'He will come to your place at 6 p.m.'

Ashim was too stunned to react.

'Are you listening?'

'Let me live in peace, Nirmal! I beg of you.'

26

When Anubhav arrived at Nirmal's house, his parents requested him to stay for at least a cup of tea. As a result, he was late by more than half an hour. Perhaps this had happened for the better, thought Anubhav. Because, by now, Ashim would've definitely reached home. It was beginning to grow dark. Along an uneven village dirt road, Anubhav and Nirmal walked towards Ashim's house.

The cowherds were bringing the cattle home from the fields. The clouds of dust rising from the cattle hooves mingled in the air. The smell of arid dust entered Anubhav's nose. It was the middle of the month of Sot, and during this time, the roads were filled with fine, dry, powdery dust. Anubhav and Nirmal's slippers were covered in a layer of dirt.

As they walked, the two heard cowbells ringing loudly, as if some temple bells were clanging in the distance. Suddenly, there came a gentle breeze carrying the smell of flowers with it—some known and some undecipherable. But the sweet smell disappeared after clinging to their noses for just a few seconds. A few birds flew idly in the sky. Perhaps they too were out on an evening stroll. Miscalculating the time, a lone firefly came out early from its home and flew above the arum leaves in the roadside ditch. Rings of smoke now spiralled up from the courtyards of a couple of households. Perhaps someone was burning thupa, or a heap of dry leaves, to drive away flies from the cattle. Or maybe they were boiling cattle feed in the manger. Swishing sounds arose from the gateways of some households. It seemed the daughters or the daughters-in-law of those households were sweeping the courtyard with bamboo brooms and had reached the edge of the courtyard in the process. And from some households, came wafting with the gentle evening breeze, the calming fragrance of dhuna incense.

A couple of passers-by headed to the market with bags made of sackcloth, to be loaded with fresh vegetables on their way back. A flock of ducks waddled across the road and entered someone's courtyard. One or two carefree chickens, standing by the side of the road, animatedly looked here and there in an inquisitive manner. Perhaps they didn't want to return to their roost early. A new-born calf sprinted spiritedly from one end of the road to the other, while two baby goats prepped for a sweet battle by raising their forelimbs. Suddenly, a bird flew overhead at high speed, screeching shrilly, as if it were a siren on an arrogant minister's convoy tearing through the heart of a busy city.

'Sir! Sir?'

Anubhav came back to reality, shaken by Nirmal's voice.

'Sir, I went to meet Ashim yesterday,' Nirmal spoke again.

'Oh, did you?'

'Yes. I told him that you would be visiting his home today,' Nirmal said before pausing. 'Sir, you would be amazed to know that Ashim answered one of your questions in just three minutes!'

'What!' exclaimed Anubhav, surprised. He was so shell-shocked that he stopped in his tracks. He knew his questions were not easy for the students of class X, but he wanted them to start thinking logically and applying themselves. *One cannot answer those questions without thinking in an original manner,* he thought. Indeed, the reason he had shared the questions was that they were so interesting that even if one was not able to answer them, one would want to keep on trying. He wanted to pique the students' interest in mathematics and promote original thinking. But he had not expected someone to solve these so quickly. Even when Nirmal had mentioned that Ashim would be able to answer the questions, Anubhav had not believed him. *Ashim must be brought back to school by hook or by crook*, thought Anubhav. With enthusiasm, he said, 'Ashim did a tremendous job!'

Nirmal smiled and boasted, 'There, didn't I tell you this yesterday? You'll see when you meet Ashim. He will solve the other two problems quickly as well,' Nirmal went on, his words pouring out with a profound sense of belief.

'Well then, when we meet him today, we must congratulate him first.'

Anubhav sir's words gave hope to Nirmal. *Yes! Ashim might come to school again!* he thought. He finally asked his teacher a question which had been bothering him, 'Sir, when I met Ashim yesterday, I noticed something, which I had observed before as well. You see, Ashim's intelligence is somewhat different than ours. Still, why did he start performing so badly in exams?'

It took some time for Anubhav to respond to Nirmal.

'See, someone might not be able to make even a ball from clay while someone else can make a beautiful statue from it. Even after knowing mathematical formulae, definitions and theorems, some students cannot solve a mathematical problem on their own, while others solve such problems easily using the same principles. Just like Ashim. These formulae, definitions and theorems are just like potter's clay, that is, raw material. Ashim worsened in his studies because of his domestic problems. Because of his situation, he couldn't learn properly. He couldn't concentrate as his mind was preoccupied with other worries. What he lacks is raw materials. I think the same reason applies to his poor performance in other subjects as well. But because he is so bright, if he studies attentively even now, he will pick up where he left off.'

Hearing Anubhav sir's words, Nirmal felt a flutter of hope. It was not impossible to get the old familiar Ashim back. He couldn't resist asking Anubhav sir another question. 'Sir, you really think Ashim will be just as good as he was in previous classes?'

Anubhav smiled. He felt Nirmal's voice was just as pure and unsullied as the peaceful twilight he had just witnessed in the village.

*

Nirmal and Anubhav stopped at the gate of Ashim's house. Darkness engulfed the entire courtyard. There was no provision for electricity here. Anubhav could see from the gateway that a small tin lamp was glowing with a flickering flame, trying to resist the enveloping darkness. Stepping onto the courtyard, Anubhav saw that a person was squatting on the veranda with his head tucked between his knees. *He must be Ashim's father,* thought Anubhav. The man's clothes were untidy. His hair had grown long and matted. Anubhav could guess that though the person was aware of their presence, he was indifferent to them. This made Anubhav feel very uncomfortable. Just as he started worrying about what to do in such an awkward situation, he heard Nirmal shouting.

'Ashim! Hey Ashim!'

Even now, with the hollering and shouting, the man didn't care to raise his head. A little later, a girl emerged.

'Hey Ajoli, where is Ashim?' asked Nirmal.

Ajoli's mouth fell open. She didn't respond to Nirmal's question, for on her veranda stood the new schoolteacher! Dumbfounded, Ajoli at first couldn't decide what to do. But when she could gather her wits, she was filled with deep shame. She ran inside the house and returned instantly with two short-legged wooden stools in her hands. She placed them on the veranda and requested shyly, 'Please take a seat, sir!'

Anubhav sat down as Nirmal and Ajoli stood next to him.

'Sir,' said Nirmal. 'This is Ajoli. She is Ashim's sister. She also studies at our school.'

'Oh, is it?' Anubhav smiled. 'Which class are you in?'

'Class VII,' the girl said in a hushed voice.

'She is very intelligent, sir,' explained Nirmal excitedly. 'She is currently ranked third in class. Earlier, it was even better. She used to come first.'

However, as he finished speaking, Nirmal felt that it would have been better not to have said the latter part as, out of embarrassment, Ajoli started scratching the muddy ground with her toenails. Like a nervous twitch.

Anubhav looked around. He could see the miserable condition the home was in. In order to make Ajoli feel comfortable, he changed the topic and asked her, 'So, where is Ashim?'

'He hasn't reached home yet.'

Immediately, a suspicion arose in Nirmal's mind, 'Does he get home this late often?'

'No, I don't know why he is so late today.'

Nirmal understood. Ashim was late deliberately. He didn't want to meet Anubhav sir. Nirmal was heartbroken.

'Is your mother also not at home?' asked Anubhav.

'No. She hasn't returned from work either,' replied Ajoli.

Anubhav didn't ask her what her mother did, as that would've made her feel more embarrassed. As time passed, it started becoming more awkward. Neither Ashim nor his mother returned. Ashim's father's presence did not make any difference. All this time, he was lying there on the veranda like a lifeless piece of wood. Perhaps he was just waiting for his son to get home to snatch away his earnings of the day. Little Ajoli was yet to learn how to greet and entertain guests. She was only replying to the questions she was being asked with her head bowed down. Anubhav soon realized that more than them, it was Ajoli who was finding the situation uncomfortable. She was too young to know how to take care of guests, and perhaps they never had any in the first place. Even if anyone came calling, maybe they never had anything in the house to offer them, not even a humble cup of tea. Perhaps, because of that too, Ajoli felt helpless and embarrassed.

The two waited and waited, and finally Anubhav and Nirmal left for home, disappointed.

27

Ashim returned home very late that night. His father was still outside on the veranda, awaiting his return. The moment his son walked in, the man berated him for being unduly late, and thereafter, taking from him some money, rushed out of the house.

By now, Ajoli had gone to bed. It was just his mother, sitting on a little stool, waiting for him in the dark house. Ashim knew that his mother wouldn't have had dinner, so he asked her to serve the food while he freshened up in the backyard.

A while later, mother and son both sat down to eat. There was no point in waiting for Ashim's father. These days, the man hardly ate in the house. And often, he didn't return home at night either. No one knew where he stayed or what he ate. His father's connection with the family was almost severed now. The only bond he had with his family was his dependence on his son's daily wages for his alcohol addiction. Ashim felt that if his father didn't have to depend on him for money, that slender link too would snap and their relationship would completely fall apart. However, in his heart of hearts, Ashim looked forward to this particular moment in the evening, because it was the only time in the entire day that his father called him by his name—Ashim. Even if it was for money. He *wanted* his father to call him 'Ashim' at least once during the hard, long day. Ashim feared that someday he might lose that comfort too.

'What are you thinking about?'

It was his mother. 'Why were you so late today?' she asked again.

'Yes . . . umm . . . I got a bit late today.'

Ashim tried to skirt around the topic. But he was hoping that his mother would give him the news that his new schoolteacher had come to meet him. However, she didn't tell him anything. *Had the teacher not come to meet me then?* As the thought crossed his mind, Ashim started to feel miserable and hollow. *Was I seriously expecting that the new teacher would come searching for me? Why was I even expecting that? To go to school again? What would I achieve by going to school?*

Ultimately, Ashim's thoughts boiled down to what he had continued to believe over the past three months. *No, there's no point in thinking about all these things.* He forcefully expelled the thoughts from his mind. Washing his hands to the side of his plate, as was the etiquette, he got up from the floor.

'Why haven't you finished your food?' his mother said, looking at his almost-untouched plate.

'Not feeling hungry at all, Ma.'

'I don't know what has happened to all of you,' she muttered sadly. 'In spite of being your mother, I don't know what's going on inside your head or even Ajoli's!' Sighing deeply, she whispered, 'Even she went to bed hungry.'

'What?' Ashim felt as if his heart had been physically twisted into a knot. 'Why? What happened to her?' he asked.

'Tell me, how can I know unless she tells me? When I returned from work, I found her lying on the cot, just crying.'

Ashim looked down, sad and confused. He noticed that his mother too was just fiddling with the rice on her plate but not really eating it. After some time, she too got up without eating anything.

Ashim kept sitting there. He felt heartbroken for his little sister. Ajoli had suffered a lot.

After a while, he went to her. Sitting beside her on the cot, he put his hand gently on her shoulders. 'Ajoli . . .' he called out to her affectionately. Ajoli remained motionless. He shook her body and called her name again, 'Ajoli . . .'

Ashim could feel that Ajoli was trembling and shivering. *She is crying.*

'Hey, what happened to you? Why are you weeping?' he asked softly.

The moment he said it, Ajoli tossed her body to face him. She looked at his eyes intently and holding one of his hands tightly, pleaded, 'Will you go back to school?'

28

Ashim couldn't figure out what was happening to him. From the moment Nirmal shared those three maths problems with him, he couldn't stop thinking about them. He'd solved one of the problems instantly. He felt if he did some more brainstorming, the solutions for the other two problems would be easy to solve as well.

Ashim caught himself thinking about all this again and immediately checked himself. He tried to persuade his mind to think of his situation: *Stop thinking about all this. There's no point for a school-dropout labourer like me to think about maths problems!*

Despite this justification, the two unsolved maths problems kept popping up in his mind. The fact was that when Nirmal shared the questions with him, Ashim had, for a moment, forgotten that he had dropped out of school. And when he'd solved the first question, his joy knew no bounds. Forgetting all his worries and woes, he'd again become the 'jewel' for a moment—Mahendra sir's jewel.

Even now, invariably, the question involving prime numbers started bothering him. *How many of the nine-digit numbers—where each of the digits from 1 to 9 is used once and only once to form the number—are prime numbers?*

Ashim was good at studies till class VII, and he had studied about prime numbers and composite numbers in class V itself. So, he had no difficulty recalling the basics. The difficulty he was facing was to stop himself from thinking about the maths problems which Nirmal gave him. Ashim looked down to see that he was lagging behind; Ramen and his other companions had already broken several tins worth of stones. Seeing this, he cursed himself: *Who would feed you? Maths or the hammer?* With time and owing to his resolve to earn money, Ashim had become an expert at breaking down the stones. Gradually, he would try his hand at other odd jobs at the quarry, such as bombing the rocks with dynamite, which would pay much more. Looking at his almost-empty tin, he got back to work in earnest.

But soon, as fate would have it, the questions began niggling at his mind once again. Suddenly, a bolt of lightning lit up the dark interiors of his brain! *Regardless of whatever nine-digit number would be formed by using each digit from 1 to 9 once and only once, the sum of the digits of such numbers would have to be $1 + 2 + 3 + \ldots + 9$, that is, $(10 \times 9)/2 = 45$. And 45 is divisible by 9. Therefore, the numbers would be divisible by 9. It implied that each number thus formed would be a composite one! Therefore, none of the numbers thus formed would be prime!*

Ashim rechecked the logic of his solution. *Yes, there's no inconsistency in his logic and line of thought!* Just as he figured out the solution to this trick question, he became breathless with excitement. Throwing the hammer onto the heap of stones, Ashim got up from his seat and started running! *School might be over by now! I can meet Nirmal outside the school gate!*

Still working in the quarry, Ramen and the others looked in the direction of Ashim's departure with surprise. 'What's gotten into him? Why is he running away from work?'

But Ashim didn't look back and instead sprinted to the school. Once near the gate, he kept pacing back and forth with restless urgency. In that moment, he felt as if time itself had stopped. *When would school get over? Uff, won't school get over today at all?* He kept ruminating while looking in the direction of the school campus.

Just then, the sound of the school bell rang through the air! He could hear the stampede of students, ready to head home. *But where's Nirmal?* With nervous excitement, Ashim craned his neck to look for his friend. But Nirmal was nowhere to be seen! Ashim got even more anxious and agitated. Just then, he spotted Nirmal amidst a group of students! As the group went past the gate, Ashim shouted out, 'Nirmal! Nirmal!'

Surprised, Nirmal walked towards his friend. But Ashim was so excited that he ran towards him. And before Nirmal could even open his mouth and scold Ashim for deliberately avoiding the teacher's visit, Ashim excitedly started speaking, 'You know, Nirmal—that maths problem you told me about, how many numbers are prime? I have found out the answer! You see, none of the numbers will be a prime number as all the numbers will be divisible by 9. See here how I have arrived at the conclusion,' he said all this in one breath and so started panting.

'Wait, wait, wait!' Nirmal spoke over the boy, equally excited. 'Rather than telling me the solution, it would be better to explain it to Anubhav sir. To be honest, only he can confirm whether you are correct or not,' saying this, Nirmal raced into the school to fetch his new teacher.

*

Anubhav and Nirmal came out hurriedly, only to find that Ashim had disappeared again. Looking at each other's faces with disappointment, they sighed.

'Seems like the idiot ran away,' said Nirmal, sadly.

'Seems like it. But what did the idiot say?' Anubhav asked Nirmal, imitating his tone.

'He said that none of the numbers would be prime. All the numbers will be divisible by 9.'

Anubhav gasped at his student's response. 'He is more of an idiot than I thought!' he added in excitement.

Hearing his teacher speak in that manner, Nirmal giggled.

*

It was as if they were embroiled in a police operation to apprehend a dangerous criminal! Anubhav and Nirmal ran to the quarry at the foot of the hill in search of Ashim. There, they saw that Ashim's companions were busy smashing stones. Everyone's collection was towering, except one boy's. Nirmal pointed at the place assigned to Ashim.

The boy's hammer was lying on a small heap of stones, but Ashim was nowhere to be seen.

29

Gradually, the days started getting warmer. Anubhav had finished his dinner a while back but hadn't gone to bed straightaway. Usually, he couldn't fall asleep without reading a few pages of a book first, a habit which filled him with a sense of tranquillity. But today, he didn't feel like reading at all.

Anubhav opened the window, put his chair beside it and sat down. He then put on a CD of Jyoti Sangeet, the classic compositions of Jyoti Prasad Agarwala who was one of the most influential artistes of modern Assam. Soon the lyrics of a melodious Jyoti Sangeet filled the air: 'O my starlet in a golden palanquin . . .'

Anubhav switched off the lights.

Occasionally, a gentle breeze came rushing through the window. The soothing effect of the wind calmed his mind and body. He could clearly see the road from his window. There was moonlight outside, and the road was speckled with the shadows of tall trees. A glint of moonlight streamed in through his window and faintly illuminated the room, giving the space a mystical ambience.

The road looked desolate at this time of the night. One or two stray dogs were running here and there. Occasionally, an old bicycle passed by, filling the air with squeaky noises. He could hear a couple of dogs chasing a bicycle, barking incessantly. And at some point, they gave up. The atmosphere became silent again, except for the sporadic sounds of bird calls.

Sitting there in the dark, a thought occurred to Anubhav. Like in many other villages, a number of things that were once common in this village too had disappeared or vanished; for instance, the jackal population! It was quite late in the night, but Anubhav couldn't hear the quintessential howl of the animal, so common in these parts. He felt pity for the jackals, which during his childhood had been central to many a story that had inspired a kind of bittersweet fear, especially at night. Mulling over this, a strange sort of sadness overcame Anubhav.

He now saw a drunkard making his way unsteadily up the road. *Perhaps Ashim's father would also be walking like this man somewhere just at this moment*, speculated Anubhav. As he thought about Ashim's father, suddenly something struck him. Something that Jilmil had said long back. Mass depression! *Can this be true? Is it because, even after so many years since Independence, on not being able to experience any meaningful progress compared to the other regions of the country—let alone the world—the people here have become deeply disenchanted with the powers that be and* have lost hope? Are people in the region experiencing some sort of mass depression? Hmm . . . come to think of it, there were news and TV reports recently which mentioned that people of a particular region had boycotted the elections en-masse. Is that a manifestation of mass depression? Perhaps, thought Anubhav. He started feeling restless.

Even now, political parties and leaders ask for votes, promising to repair roads. But this, alongside basic means of communication, drinking water and other essential services should have been the bare minimum that the governments should have delivered to the citizens. Yet, these still remain burning issues, which leaders promise to 'solve' by shouting out eloquently written speeches at election rallies. So many years after Independence, what should have been our political issues at this point in time? And what are our issues, huh? The greed of cunning, corrupt and incompetent leaders have resulted in the misery of the public.

Anubhav reminisced about the day when he'd visited Ashim's house, and he had seen the boy's father. There he was, wearing filthy clothes, squatting on the veranda with his head tucked between his knees—as if in a posture of utter defeat. It appeared as if he didn't want to annoy anyone with his existence. Anubhav understood that here was a man who was caught in the throes of abject despair. So how could he hate a man like that? Anubhav knew that there was a distinct difference between a person who consumed alcohol for fun and one who drank to drown his sorrows. He remembered Jilmil mentioning that alcohol consumption had increased a lot in the village and with that, alcohol–related crimes had risen as well. Hmm . . . there must be some connection between this and the mass depression *issue she spoke about,* he thought. *But whatever the reason, if a family member got caught up in this terrible addiction, the rest of the household suffered alongside that person as well.*

It was true. Whatever the reason behind Ashim's father's dependency on the bottle, the truth was that he'd slipped into a downward spiral. And this degradation had brought upon doom on his entire family. And it was exactly on this point that Anubhav's opinion differed from others: he didn't set store by the theory that the social circumstances which had pushed Ashim's father to take to drink would magically disappear one fine day, and then from that day onwards he would give up his addiction, which in turn would then assuage all his family's problems. However, this was exactly what political parties and some 'intellectuals' espoused. In fact, to get to the root of this issue, one could use Ashim and other children like him as case studies to analyse why children like him drop out of school early and what the root causes behind their miseries were. Then, on the basis of such analyses, meaningful governmental and non-governmental schemes could be implemented. However, the intention behind such policies should be sound and there should be concerted efforts to avoid fooling the people by claiming to overturn their fortunes overnight. Because for such problems, there can be no shortcuts. And these policies and plans are definitely long-drawn processes that take time to show visible results.

Hmm . . . but till then, what would become of Ashim and countless others like him? wondered Anubhav as he thought about this issue.

Would Ashim wait for the 'promised' good days to come without doing anything? Should young people like him watch their futures drift away while so-called intellectuals and politicians pontificate on their fates and come up with clever theories on how to help this vulnerable section of society? In fact, many of these so-called leaders and philosophers made themselves profitable in the knowledge market by dissecting the miseries of Ashim and others like him. And on the other hand, most of the political leaders and parties did not want to implement any long-term welfare programme in a meaningful way. Not that the policies had any deep thought or research or even honesty backing them. And this lack of honesty added to the lack of initiative among the policymakers.

Thinking about this, Anubhav suddenly became highly sceptical: *Is there anyone who really thinks about and feels the pain and plight of people like Ashim?*

Anubhav reasoned that because of these reasons, unlike many intellectuals, he couldn't ignore the personal efforts of a demoralized person trying his best to get himself out of his misery. *After all, there is no point teaching a family that is trapped precariously in the middle of a flood, about the causes of the flood or about the measures to be taken to prevent calamities at that point in time. Or worse, making them wait in the water till a policy rescues them. What if the poor family, stuck in such a terrible situation, is, in fact, persuaded? Along with their hopes, they will then drown in the flood water.*

Anubhav pondered over the issues for a long time in the darkness. He concluded that if there were some political parties and leaders or intellectuals honestly engaged in the effort to improve the conditions of downtrodden families, it is very much commendable. Their thoughts and efforts will surely benefit society at large. In spite of that, the underprivileged has to make an effort himself at personal level to overcome his problems. *Yes, if one stays idle believing in abstract ideas and ideals, it will only create dangers and these dangers will ultimately destroy the person and others will witness that destruction from a safe distance. That is why, if the conditions of Ashim's family were to improve, the child must return to school again. And his father must give up drinking.*

*

A gust of wind blew through the bamboo grove. A solitary breeze put a stop to Anubhav's free flowing thoughts. Distracted, he now saw someone walk through the gate leading into his courtyard. *Who has come at this hour? Who could it be?*

The person staggered while walking, swaying from side to side. *Could he be Ashim's father? Hmm . . . but why would Ashim's father come to meet me of all people, and that too at this hour?* After all, the other day, when he visited Ashim's house, the man didn't utter a single word or even receive them as guests at his home out of courtesy!

The man staggered forward now. Anubhav noticed that he had a shawl wrapped around him even in this blistering heat. He leaned forward and peered out into the courtyard, but couldn't recognize the face of the stranger at all!

'Rat–a–tat!'

Anubhav heard a loud knock on the backdoor of the house. *Should I even open the door?* Anubhav wondered, anxious.

'Rat–a–tat!'

Just then, there was another insistent knock.

'Open up, please!' urged the man, his voice slurring.

'Rat–a–tat! Rat–a–tat! Rat–a–tat!'

More unsteady knocks followed, louder this time. The man was now loudly banging his fists on the door.

Switching off the CD player, Anubhav got up and walked to the door. Cautiously, he put his hand on the door bolt and then yanked it open.

Anubhav was startled when he saw who his visitor was.

The stranger was indeed Ashim's father! The man was clearly intoxicated and unable to stand up straight as he swayed unsteadily on the step.

Before Anubhav could react, he saw Kamal, the son of his landlord, sprinting towards them. There was a stick in his hand.

'Are you the new teacher?' asked Ashim's father.

Before Anubhav could say anything, Kamal rushed towards them and dealt a violent blow on the man's leg with the stick, as if he were a stray dog!

'Aaaaaahhh!' Ashim's father howled in pain. He massaged his leg with his hand.

'You drunkard!' screamed Kamal. 'Why are you creating a nuisance here?' He grabbed the man by the neck and started pushing him towards the main road.

'Let . . . let me go,' said Ashim's father, struggling. 'I . . . I have come to say something to the teacher . . .' said the man, gasping for breath. It seemed as if he was exhausted.

'What nonsense! You have come to talk to the teacher at midnight?' asked Kamal scornfully and proceeded to deal another blow, now on the man's back.

Anubhav stood shell-shocked. Bewildered, he kept staring at this attack with his mouth agape.

By now, pushing and dragging the man, Kamal had moved him out of the path that led to the doorway and on to the deserted night road. In the moonlit night, Anubhav saw Ashim's father leaving their house, limping unsteadily. He noticed that the man's shawl was not on his body.

'So what if I drink? Does that mean I can't talk to a good man?' complained Ashim's father loudly into the dark night.

A good man? Anubhav was confused and conflicted. *Did he mean me? And what did the man want to say to me?*

As Anubhav moved to close the door, he saw that Ashim's father's shawl was lying abandoned on his doorstep.

30

The sun had set a little while back and daylight was fading fast. It would soon start getting dark. By now, Ashim's companions had already left for home. Before it got really dark, he too needed to finish his work for the day and head home. Today, Ashim was feeling quite tired. Over the past few days, he had taken up an additional task that required a lot of effort from him. He was tasked with the additional job of planting dynamite on rocks, and this had to be generally done either early morning or late in the evening when there were very few people at the quarry.

Dynamite was used to blast the gigantic rocks into smaller pieces. Even after that, the big chunks that remained were still rather big in size. Using large hammers, those pieces had to be manually broken into smaller, more manageable stones. Ashim and his companions broke those small pieces of rocks into stone chips. Dibakar, the contractor, would then load those into small trucks ready for transportation.

The process involved first choosing a huge rock on the hill for blasting. Since these rocks cling firmly to the hillside, three or four boys would dig and loosen the soil around the chosen rock using long iron digging bars. Gradually, when the bond of the rock with the attached soil would weaken, the boys, with the help of digging bars and crowbars, would pierce the layer of dry, red top soil. Once the bars would strike deeper at the slightly wet layer of soil, the hill would no longer be able to bear the load of the rock. This would topple the rock, sending it rolling downhill. However, this also meant that earthquake–like tremors would be felt in the surrounding areas.

And this aspect of the job made Ashim very distraught. He felt the entire exercise was akin to snatching away a baby from the warmth of the mother's bosom. Gathering speed, the big rock would roll downhill till it inevitably came to a stop at the bottom of the hill. It would then lie there like a dead, motionless object. And in the space from where the rock had dislodged, a gaping hole would remain. A fresh red spot would shine there, like a flesh wound. Seeing these empty voids, Ashim would feel extremely sad. He couldn't share these feelings with his companions. If they ever heard him voice these thoughts, they would roll on the floor laughing, mocking and teasing him. After all, this type of talk or having feelings didn't fit into their rock–hard life. And Ashim understood that. He understood it very clearly. But he also held a whole world inside his heart. His own internal world. And he could not show this to anyone else. In fact, he deliberately didn't want to share an iota of this world with anyone. If anyone tried to trespass into his world, he would just run away from that person.

Ashim wanted to undertake the task of planting dynamite on the rocks by himself. On his own, all alone.

This evening, as he walked towards the rock to be blasted, he felt as if it were a patient spreadeagled on a hospital bed. They had already made four holes in the rock yesterday, places where they would insert dynamite. As he approached it, Ashim felt like touching the rock affectionately for one last time. He touched the rock gently with both hands. Thereafter, he inserted a dynamite stick into one hole. He took out a matchbox from his pocket and tried to light a matchstick, but the wind was too rough. Finally, after many tries, lighting the wick of the dynamite with a burning matchstick, Ashim ran away from the spot. As he was running away, he heard the explosive going off loudly. The shrieks of terrorized birds cut through the air.

Ashim stopped at the foot of the hill and turned to look back.

He was thunderstruck, for he saw some policemen rushing towards him.

But Ashim didn't make any attempt to run away. He simply stood there, motionless.

31

Occasionally, Ashim returned home late. So, when Ashim didn't return on time that evening, his mother was not worried. However, when it became too dark outside, she became scared. Pacing in and out of the house, she stepped out on to the road a couple of times as well to see whether he was on his way or not, but Ashim was nowhere to be seen.

Ashim's father, too, was sitting on the veranda, waiting for Ashim. He'd been waiting for a long time now, and was starting to feel annoyed. He was becoming restless. *Why is he late today? He's never been this late. It is already getting too dark.* He had not tasted a drop of alcohol that day, and it was becoming quite unbearable for him. Being the addict that he was, he was itching to run to the country liquor shop with today's earnings.

Now terribly anxious, Ashim's mother nudged her husband to go in search of their son a number of times. But he didn't respond. Knowing his temper and his tendency to fly off the handle, she didn't want to push him too hard. But inside, she was starting to get agitated. She nurtured a sustained sense of sorrow on account of Ashim. It pained her that Ashim, who used to be a class topper, had to drop out of school due to his circumstances. Her sorrow increased manifold on having to see him toil at the quarry. She felt guilty for the suffering Ashim had to undergo.

At last, unable to sit quietly, Ashim's mother lost her patience. She roared at her husband, 'Even a cow starts mooing when she can't find her calf! But you won't budge from there and continue to sit motionless while Ashim is god knows where?'

But the man didn't respond. He kept sitting on the veranda, dozing.

32

Ashim couldn't comprehend why the police was keeping him in custody. After all, he'd been planting the dynamite sticks for a while now. As usual, Dibakar, the contractor, had given him the explosives in the afternoon before leaving the site. *Did the police arrest me because I had the explosives on me when they caught me? But then, rocks are shattered only when they are dislodged with such explosives; it's common knowledge. So why did they arrest me today?* he wondered.

Ashim was scared. Whenever the police approached them, his companions and he would make a run for it. If ever the police visited the village to make any inquiries, the kids would observe everything with excitement, but from a safe vantage point. Today was different somehow. The police had taken him in.

Ashim had heard people mention that the police station was some sixteen kilometres away from their village. He had never travelled such a long distance without his family. And although they hadn't handcuffed

him, Ashim still found the demeanour of the police
intimidating. And why wouldn't he? After all, he'd heard
that the police would thrash people severely in the lock-
up. Ashim wondered whether he would be beaten up too
and if he had committed any big crime unwittingly. He
had been beaten up by his father on many occasions and,
of course, Mahendra sir had whacked him at school. *But
the police will beat me up much more severely than Mahendra
sir*, Ashim shuddered. It was also said that the police
became more menacing at night after consuming alcohol.

In anticipation of said police brutality, his heart started
thumping rapidly. He felt as if his throat was parched. He
wished for a glass of water. He experienced hunger pangs
too. *But food aside, I might not even get to sleep!* he thought.
He would probably have to spend the night on the bench,
getting bitten by mosquitoes. His mother's face appeared
repeatedly before his eyes. Ajoli's too. *Have they heard the
news?* He was surprised that at this hour of crisis, another
face floated before his eyes—that of Nirmal's! *Has Nirmal
come to know about this?*

As soon as he remembered Nirmal, he remembered
yet another person—the new teacher! The person was
unfamiliar to him. But Ashim had heard Nirmal speak
highly of him on several occasions. This person had even
taken the pains to visit his house to meet him. And what
had he done in return? He'd spent that evening sitting at
the top of the hill, staying away from home to avoid the
new teacher. From the hilltop, everything appeared small,
even miniature, be it the trees or the houses. Even human
beings were indistinguishable from such a distance. That

day, when Ashim was sitting on the hill, avoiding Nirmal and the new teacher, he'd experienced a weird sort of feeling. The vast expanse of nature had overwhelmed him. He realized he was a small entity in comparison to the vastness of nature. His sorrows were so insignificant when compared to the limitlessness of nature. That day, he'd experienced a strange kind of emotion. He felt a little detached—as if he were far removed from everyone—be it his father, his mother or Ajoli.

'Hey, you! Yes, dial Dibakar's number!' With a shrill command, a constable handed him a mobile phone.

Ashim looked at the constable helplessly. He didn't know how to make a phone call. In fact, he had never made a phone call in his life! But he was too frightened to say it out loud.

'I . . . I . . . sir . . . I don't know how to make a call,' Ashim blurted out hesitantly.

All of a sudden, a tight slap landed on his cheek. Ashim's vision blurred from the sheer force of the hit.

'Then tell me the number of your boss,' said the constable as he snatched the phone away and continued to glare at him.

This time, Ashim was even more frightened to disclose that he didn't even know the phone number of his supervisor. He just broke down stones and waited for Dibakar to pay him the money, after which he would go home. That was it. The need for a phone number never arose in this transaction.

'Why aren't you speaking, you buffoon?' roared the constable, hurling abuses at him.

'I . . . I honestly don't know his number.'

Another tight slap landed on his other cheek. This time, Ashim was ready for it. Still, it hurt even more this time.

'Why does your boss keep changing his phone number so frequently, huh? Doesn't he know that he has to pay *hafta*, which is due every month?'

Ashim observed that while speaking just two sentences, the constable had used four to five obscene words. He also learned a word which he had never heard before: Hafta! *Hafta needs to be paid every month? But why am I being beaten up just because Dibakar hasn't paid them the hafta? And now he can't be reached? How is that my fault?*

In this inexplicable situation, Ashim was petrified with terror and anxiety. His mind was bogged down with questions that played in a loop: who would rescue him from this terrible situation? Who? His mother couldn't come to the police station so far away from their village to rescue him, could she? He couldn't even expect anything from his father, who by now was long gone from their lives, although he was physically present at their house. He was oblivious to the family's fortunes or misfortunes. No one in his family knew anything about the world inside their father's mind. They didn't even know where he stayed at night on most days or what he ate, if at all.

But things were not like this before.

Suddenly, he recalled an old incident.

It was either in class II or class III; he couldn't remember. But it was evening, and for some reason, he'd picked up the family's only bottle of kerosene. Somehow, the bottle had slipped through his fingers and fallen to the ground. The kerosene had spilled everywhere. When he picked up the bottle, he realized that only a little bit of kerosene remained in it. Since they were poor, it was hard for his parents to buy another bottle of kerosene, and his mother had become extremely angry with him. She had chased him, punching him on the back. And as soon as the second punch had landed on his back, Ashim had sprinted off and stepped on to the road.

As he'd put his first step on the road, he remembered taking a deep breath, he had wondered where he could go. He couldn't even fathom returning home till his mother's anger had subsided, that much was clear to Ashim. He remembered going to a familiar shop nearby. Not really a shop—more of a roadside stand really. Quite small. It stocked some things like biscuits, chocolates, lozenges, hair ribbons and other sundry items. The shopkeeper had put up a makeshift bench outside by nailing a wooden plank on to two bamboo posts. So, Ashim had gone and sat there, waiting for his mother's fury to subside.

The old shopkeeper was surprised to find the boy in front of his shop at that late hour. Still, he'd chatted with the boy. Gradually, the number of customers had started to trickle down and, after a while, there was no one left there other than the boy and the shopkeeper. It was completely dark. Still, Ashim could not muster the courage to return home and face the ire of his mother. Perhaps he'd thought then that his father too would get angry at him. The old shopkeeper insisted that the boy return home. Another bout of anxiety had started terrorizing Ashim. Because it was time to close the shop, where would he go after it was closed for the day? Already, the road was deserted. Jackals had started to howl too. As he was absorbed in those anxious thoughts, suddenly someone hugged him and picked him up from behind and said, 'Let's go home.'

That was his father!

And then his father had walked the entire stretch to his house, hugging Ashim close to him. Upon reaching home, he'd scolded Ashim's mother, saying that she did not have the slightest affection for her son!

Now, in the cold police station, Ashim yearned to hear his father's affectionate words again. He wished that his father would come to the police station, hug him from behind, hold him close and utter those caring and affectionate words again, 'Let's go home.'

Ashim felt as if something had choked his throat. Day-long toil, thirst and hunger, and the ill treatment by the police constable had crushed him to the bone. Just then, he heard the bell in the police station clock ringing. Ashim counted: one, two, three . . . It was 10 p.m. Sitting down on the station's bench, Ashim closed his eyes and resting his head on the wall, he fell asleep.

*

'Ashim!'

'Hey Ashim!' someone called out softly.

Who is calling out to me so affectionately? Deuta? Oh, how long has it been since Deuta has spoken to me so lovingly? Is it a dream?

'Ashim!'

The boy tried to open his eyelids a little, but closed them again.

'Hey Ashim!'

Such a caring and affectionate voice! I could die for such affection! This is such a beautiful dream.

But this was not a dream! Not a dream! Someone was indeed holding him close and was calling out his name.

'Let's go home,' the voice said.

Rubbing his eyes, Ashim jerked himself awake forcibly. A stranger was holding him close.

Who is this person? No—no—I have seen him somewhere—I've met him somewhere. But where? Ashim thought as he kept gazing at the person incredulously.

'You've failed to recognize me, haven't you?' A warm and loving smile spread across the person's face—a smile that could pull at anyone's heartstrings.

Suddenly, it struck him.

That's a nice name you've got! A sentence he'd heard before!

Ashim remembered everything! Yes, he could finally recognize the person! He had met him four months ago, on the day on which his results had been declared. The day Mahendra sir had slapped him and declared: 'You are ruined!'

'Once he was the topper in his class!' Mahendra sir had said it to this very person!

Mahendra master had slapped him hard and left. And that person had gently asked, 'What's your name?'

'A–Ashim!' he had replied in a broken voice, filled with sorrow and humiliation.

'That's a nice name you've got!' the man had said, before hurriedly leaving for the gate.

Yes, yes, he remembered everything now! Everything was still fresh in his memory and, because of such small acts of kindness, he was still alive now. Still breathing.

'You still can't recognize me, right?' the man asked affectionately.

Ashim nodded. He'd finally remembered who this person was. Ashim felt like crying. He had not cried for a long time. Yes, it's okay. It is okay to cry before this man. Tears started rolling down his cheeks in rivulets.

'I'm your new teacher!' said Anubhav.

What? This man is the new teacher that Nirmal mentioned? Could this be true?

Wonder, emotions, nervous excitement—all overwhelmed Ashim at once, and he started weeping mournfully, his head buried in Anubhav's chest.

33

Tired and demoralized, Ashim lay motionless like a piece of wood on the cot the entire night. The storm that had hit his life at such a tender age yesterday should not have let him sleep, but the tremendous amount of sorrow and exhaustion paralysed his consciousness and his ability to think. As if, in the real sense of the term, he'd died after reaching home. It was only when a ray of sunlight passing through his window fell on his face that he'd woken up.

His father was not on the cot. It was midnight by the time Anubhav sir had dropped him home, but his father was nowhere to be seen. *Did Deuta even know what had happened last night? Didn't his heart ache when he found out that his son was assaulted by the police?* Such thoughts assailed Ashim, making him despondent.

No, Ashim didn't have the luxury of harbouring such emotional thoughts in his life any more. Forcing aside all these unnecessary emotions, Ashim returned to the harsh reality.

What would he do now?

While returning home from the police station, Anubhav sir told him something about the quarry. According to him, the quarry was being run illegally as the owner, Paresh, had not taken the necessary government clearances and permissions to run it. And anyway, a quarry shouldn't have been operational on that hill in the first place, Anubhav sir had said.

'Why illegal, even a legal quarry should not be there!'

According to him, the hill was situated in a geographically critical location. If the hill were to get destroyed, the river running around the foot of the hill would change its course, and this would mean that eventually the village would get flooded and washed away by the river. Therefore, in the opinion of Anubhav sir, even if the government gave permission for a legal quarry in that location in future, the villagers should vehemently protest against such a decision.

It'd become clear to Ashim that the quarry owned by Paresh was running illegally thanks to his nexus with the local police station. For that, Dibakar deposited a certain sum—a hafta—at the police station regularly every month. And when there was a delay in depositing the money or if the amount given was less than what was the norm, the police would pick up one or two labourers, like Ashim, in order to make Paresh and Dibakar toe the line. They would threaten to close the quarry and make other such intimidations. In the tug of war between the police and the quarry management, it was workers like Ashim who got crushed.

Anubhav sir had further said that the main ingredient that they used while planting the explosives on the rocks, which they called salt or masala at the quarry, was actually gelatine. And that meant real explosives. 'Terrorists use those to build bombs!' Anubhav sir had said. 'It would be very dangerous if these things were to fall into the hands of miscreants.' Anubhav sir had also inferred that the owners of a certain legal quarry or labourers of such mines, without the knowledge of the owner, had sold these explosives to the owners of other illegal mines, like the one run by Paresh and Dibakar.

'There must be some black market for these sorts of explosives, you know, Ashim,' he'd explained.

'If mine owners like Paresh can procure these explosives so easily, so can terrorists! Therefore, it's vital that the police put a stop to this illegal process.'

It was clear that it was not a difficult task to locate the source from which explosives had been illegally bought, and perhaps the police department knew about it too. But due to their systemic corruption, they didn't take any action.

After hearing all this information, Ashim couldn't bring himself to go to that illegal quarry to work again. If he were to go there, he knew he would hurt Anubhav sir. For the first time after a long period, Ashim didn't want to do something lest it hurt a certain person. As this thought crossed his mind, the young boy couldn't decide whether to feel good about it or not. He was conflicted.

Several other thoughts attacked his mind at once. If he didn't break down stones for a living, what would he do now? Even after a lot of thinking, he couldn't decide on any alternative to earning a wage to support his family. Yet he could also see a glimmer of hope: Anubhav sir. In fact, his teacher would come to their house today! And this time, he wouldn't run away and hide. After all, how could he run away from the person who had rescued and brought him home from the police station at midnight?

Even in the middle of such a terrible incident in his life, this person joked while pacifying him yesterday, saying, 'You were running away from me! What will you do now?' Anubhav sir had tried to make the atmosphere lighter by saying that it was he who had got Ashim arrested because he kept running away. Ashim realized that, in fact, it was Anubhav who had truly imprisoned him with his caring nature.

Ashim was looking forward to his teacher coming to meet him; he felt happy for a change. It had been a while since his mind was filled with such excitement. Anubhav sir had even promised to bring a present for him! Actually, it was a prize for being able to solve two out of the three maths problems he had given in class. Yes, the same Ashim whom Mahendra sir had slapped mercilessly for going astray had solved these problems. The same Ashim whom the police had apprehended, beaten up and detained in the police station. Today, Anubhav sir would be awarding a prize to that same Ashim!

Last night, after handing him over to his crying mother, Anubhav sir asked him gently, smiling broadly, 'What happened to the third problem?'

Ashim had been surprised. His mother had also gazed at him, puzzled. *Ma!* His teary-eyed, distressed mother had kept staring at this unknown person, mouth agape, who had brought her son back from the police station. Everything had become riddle-like and confusing for her. In hindsight, it was funny, seeing the person talking about maths problems in the middle of the night with the accused, who had just returned from the police station. In all this, even his sobbing mother forgot to cry.

Ashim now pieced everything together. He could easily guess that it must have been Nirmal who informed Anubhav sir about his arrest. And it was definitely Nirmal who had notified Anubhav sir that two of his three maths problems had been solved.

Ashim took a deep breath. It seemed that even if at times one might feel like drowning oneself in the ocean of sorrow and lose oneself in the darkness of hopelessness, one couldn't give in to such feelings of despondency. Friends like Nirmal wouldn't allow that and people like Anubhav sir would be there too, ready to dispel darkness from one's life.

Last night, when Ashim had introduced his mother to Anubhav sir, she had immediately fallen to the ground and touched his feet, hugging his legs. 'You are not a mere human—' she had sobbed.

Shocked at this and without letting her finish her words, Anubhav sir had jumped backwards. He spoke to her with a gentle smile on his face, 'Eh . . . do you take me for some ghost?'

Anubhav sir had lit up their minds previously made gloomy by the sudden misfortune of Ashim being arrested. Ashim's mind too was filled with inexplicable emotions for his teacher. Was it gratitude? No, this emotion couldn't be explained or contained by that single, uncomplicated word. At the same time, he was hurt by his father's behaviour. The man was not in the house yesterday when Ashim returned from the police station. Under normal circumstances, it should have been the child's parent who should have rescued and brought him back from the police station. In fact, it was his father who was responsible for the circumstances leading to all this misfortune.

Ashim, now lying in his cot, heard his mother shouting at his father to her heart's content while she swept the courtyard. Ashim looked at the adjacent cot; Ajoli was fast asleep. He felt terrible for his little sister. She had endured a lot because of the circumstances in their home. Nowadays, she remained constantly unhappy and in a depressed state. How Ashim wished that he could make her happy somehow!

All of a sudden, Ashim didn't feel like dwelling on gloomy thoughts. Last night, when Anubhav sir had asked him about the third mathematical problem, he'd just stared at him blankly. Earlier, thinking about the sums would have conjured mixed emotions in him: one moment he'd feel good, but the very next moment, it would make him think of school, and he'd feel blue.

Perhaps now that he'd actually met Anubhav sir, he could get around to solving the third and final maths problem.

And so, Ashim escaped into the world of maths, far removed from the sufferings of the real world.

34

Lying in his bed, Anubhav was thinking about what had transpired the previous night. It was a big tragedy for Ashim to be arrested and taken to the police station at such a young age. He knew that children at this age were naturally scared of the police. And then to have been tied up and thrashed! If Anubhav hadn't reached on time to rescue him, the boy would have spent the whole night in lock-up. He would have suffered more harassment there, for sure. Anubhav shuddered; he had heard a lot about the horrid atmosphere in police stations at night.

No! I cannot let a boy like Ashim be lost for good, Anubhav thought. He was certain that today, when he'd visit Ashim's house, the boy would be there. Anubhav sighed. Despite the disasters that had befallen Ashim, Anubhav actually thought the boy was lucky, for he had a loyal friend like Nirmal. Even if Ashim often tended to get lost in blind alleys, Nirmal had been there, trying continuously to bring him back on track.

Even yesterday, it was Nirmal who informed him about Ashim being apprehended by the police. The moment Nirmal had overheard his parents talking about the incident, he'd called Anubhav immediately from his father's phone. Anubhav took a deep breath. He knew he had not given his phone number to Nirmal or to any of his students. So, in order to get his number, Nirmal must have had to call numerous people. Anubhav recalled the anxiousness in his voice when the boy had called. He had asked Anubhav repeatedly, 'Sir, will the police beat him up?'

It was past midnight by the time he was able to get Ashim released. Although Anubhav had wanted to ring up Nirmal immediately to give him the news, he didn't want to disturb Nirmal's parents. However, Nirmal's father had called him a while later to ask about Ashim and his current situation.

'Sir, Nirmal is yet to go to bed,' he'd said. 'But for him, sleep is so essential that . . .' The man had paused midway without completing the sentence. He continued after a pause, 'Actually, I too should have gone with you. Nirmal also urged me to go. But I . . .'

The man had paused again.

Anubhav knew what the man was trying to say. Actually, he had not thought about it that way at all! After all, who was he to judge? Even Ashim's own father had not shown any concern. Shockingly, he was absent when Anubhav returned with Ashim from the police station. Even Ashim's mother had cribbed and cried about it last night.

Rat–a–tat! Rat–a–tat! Rat–a–tat!

Anubhav's thoughts were interrupted by the sound of banging on the door. *Who is it at this early hour?* he thought, tossing in bed. He had been feeling a bit uncomfortable in this rented house since that night's incident with Ashim's father. And now again, hearing the sound of the insistent knocking on the door, he became alert. *Could it be Ashim's father again? That day, the shawl had fallen off his shoulders. Had he come to collect the shawl?* Anubhav sighed. If Kamal, the landlord's son, got to know about it, another problematic confrontation might happen again. Hurriedly getting off the bed, Anubhav opened the door.

'Oh . . .'

It *was*, in fact, Ashim's father at the doorway! The man kept standing silently in front of the door. Anubhav, shocked, could not decide what to say to the man. A few seconds passed very uneasily. Anubhav now became a bit apprehensive, lest any unpleasant incident occur again. Not finding the courage to invite the man inside, into his room, Anubhav hurriedly went to fetch the shawl. He now extended his hand to return the wrap to the man, hoping for some relief in this awkward exchange.

Ashim's father took the shawl but kept staring at Anubhav. The latter felt as if the man's eyes were about to brim over with tears. 'Oh . . .' Anubhav realized that the man had not come today in an inebriated state. He was completely sober.

'I didn't come here to collect my shawl,' saying this, Ashim's father got down from the veranda and went out

186 Mrinal Kalita

through the gate. Anubhav, speechless, just kept staring and watched him disappear into the distance.

Why did he come here? To express his gratitude? What did he want? The man remained a riddle for Anubhav.

35

Ashim felt a bit uncomfortable as he opened the packet containing the prize given by his new teacher. Anubhav sir had brought all the books of class X, notebooks for each subject, pens, pencils, a geometry box and almost every item that a student needed. This had been packaged as a 'prize' for Ashim. All the items were brand new. Looking at the new books and other school-related items, Ashim was shell-shocked. He remembered the time he was berated in front of the whole class for not having a single textbook.

Though he couldn't find the words to say anything in response, Ashim could comprehend the significance behind this gift.

Just this afternoon, something had transpired that had made him realize this. His mother was present at home, and Ajoli had gone out to play with her friends; as usual, no one knew about their father's whereabouts. On seeing the generous items brought by the teacher,

Ashim's mother wiped her free-flowing tears with the edge of her chador. The boy could feel that his mother was very happy today; she'd seen a ray of hope.

Ashim was befuddled. He kept sitting on the cot with his head bowed. On seeing him sitting like that, Anubhav asked him, gently, 'What happened?'

Out of courtesy, Ashim raised his head and looked at the man, who found it difficult to decipher the boy's intense gaze. 'You have to start going to school from tomorrow,' he said.

Ashim blinked and gazed at Anubhav's face. *He wants to revive the spirit, restore my long-lost hopes*, thought Ashim.

The room was silent. Every time Anubhav met Ashim, he felt the boy didn't want to talk. He always remained absorbed in his own thoughts. He was unnaturally solemn for his age. Yet, if Nirmal was to be believed, Ashim had not been like this before. He was innocent, carefree and had played with the other children, had fun with them, and laughed with them to his heart's content. Anubhav could tell that Ashim was a very emotional and sensitive boy. *Maybe his heart is filled with pride and self-respect. Maybe he doesn't want to share his sufferings and sorrows with anyone. Perhaps he withdraws into himself—but he must be brought out of that shell.*

Anubhav now asked Ashim's mother to leave for work. He knew she was already running late. So, offering both of them tea, she left in haste.

Now alone with his teacher, Ashim felt very awkward.

During the silkworm's chrysalis, when it is time for the adult moth to come out of the pupa, there are bound to be some uneasy struggles, thought Anubhav. He knew that even if Ashim didn't say anything himself, he would definitely listen to what Anubhav was going to say.

Anubhav now started to talk to the boy.

'Problems are a part of life. And they will keep coming relentlessly, one after another. Everyone has their share of worries. You've experienced your share of problems already. Big ones. Huge ones. Troubles which you should not have faced at this young age. Usually, parents should be able to shield children from these kinds of difficulties. They should ensure their children feel free enough to play and study without having to shoulder such burdens.'

Anubhav went on to explain that Ashim's mother tried to do that, but his father didn't. And there might be reasons for it. However, with time, things got worse, and now his father himself had become a challenge for them. These problems, however, must be solved. 'We have to put in serious efforts to solve these difficulties for your father. And these efforts could be made simultaneously in different ways,' said Anubhav.

Anubhav continued to explain the situation to Ashim.

It is easy for some intellectuals or political parties to analyse the plight of underprivileged families like that of Ashim's on the basis of their own ideologies. Who knows, they might also be able to discover the actual causes of such misery. However, here is what becomes important: government initiatives. If the government doesn't do anything after identifying the causes, then everything fails. And if the authorities don't follow through, it is the responsibility of social and political leaders to stir up movements to protest the officials' inaction.

Perhaps the underprivileged might also participate in such protest movements. But while doing this, the disadvantaged people who participate in such people's movements need to be wary of crafty politicians who could turn such beneficial movements into instruments to further their own vested political agenda. Moreover, protests and agitations require time to yield results. People should not expect that problems and issues would die down within a week or a month or even a year. Added to that, resolutions might not even move in the direction in which people like Ashim would like them to proceed. Hence, they should be careful and discerning, and they should not just surrender their future to the leaders, parties, intellectuals or governments and sit idle, just wishing for things to get better.

Let all of these people do their jobs sincerely with utmost honesty. Perhaps then the results would show, and good days will come for the likes of Ashim. However, till then, one cannot push the pause button as if in a science fiction novel or movie.

And for the underprivileged, they should not just sign-off on their fates and put them in the hands of the powerful. They should not think that since they themselves are not responsible for their miseries, they will not be able to do anything to clear away those miseries. They must make concerted efforts to improve their own lot. Occasionally, in such terrible situations, people often find it easy to convince and self-deceive themselves with this sort of convoluted logic—that whatever is happening is just fate unfolding and they have no agency. This just leads to the disadvantaged becoming pawns that are sacrificed with impunity in the game of political chess.

If someone expects to pause and only live life *after* their problems die down, then it's faulty thinking. Ultimately, what the Buddha said in his parable of the mustard seed is true. It is impossible to find a home without sorrow, and collecting even a handful of mustard seeds from a house where suffering or death has not entered is impossible. And even in these trying circumstances, one must carry on one's duties and continue to live life. In fact, one should discharge one's duties even more sincerely in difficult times. And one might not even succeed, but there is dignity in defeat too. Even after playing sincerely, a football team may get defeated in a match. So should they accept defeat and stop playing altogether? Should they lose dignity by taking such an escapist route?

Even at the face of an ultimate disaster, people should collect ammunition to stand up for a fight. 'People should be earnest and try their best, relentlessly, every single day, and by dint of their own efforts, put their lives back on track,' continued Anubhav. 'Let me tell you a story,' he said.

'There was once a man who drank all the time and abused his family members, creating nuisance. The man had two sons that grew up in that unfortunate, unhealthy and disturbing environment. In due course of time, the elder son grew up to be an immoral man just like his father while the younger son grew up to be an honest and diligent person. Everyone was curious as to how it was possible that, in spite of growing up in the exact same environment, two very different personalities developed. One day, a man asked the elder son, "Why have you become like this?" To which the elder son replied, "What can I do? From a very tender age, I have seen my father behave like this." The man then asked the same question to the younger son. The boy too replied the same: "From a very tender age, I have seen my father behave like this!" So, you see, Ashim, it is not disaster that shapes a man's fortune; but it is how a man *responds* to that tragedy that shapes his future. It is not that air puts resistance and impedes a bird's flight, but that it is with the help of this resistance of the air that a bird can fly. Ashim, in spite of your innumerable sorrows and misfortunes, one thing that you have to remember to carry with you, more than your fortunate friends, is that you must grow up into a good man, a virtuous man, a good citizen who can contribute to society positively and meaningfully.'

Anubhav explained gently that it was a crime not to use one's calibre or to waste it, despite the circumstances. 'You solved two maths problems beautifully with your ingenuity while you were going through so many troubles. Who knows, with the same creativity, you could go on to discover some important things in areas of maths or science tomorrow! Who knows, an honest, virtuous and talented boy like Nirmal might discover something big in medical science that could benefit thousands of people on their death beds. And then there's Atanu! He might make some novel contributions in the field of literature. You children are the future and the torch of these possibilities must be kept burning.'

Ashim listened, enraptured by his teacher.

'My boy,' said Anubhav, 'because of all these reasons, you must go to school and enrol again.'

Anubhav also reassured Ashim that he would think about an alternative means of livelihood for him that won't interfere with his studies. 'Till the time it is accomplished, I will even lend you the necessary money.'

By now, it was late, and Ashim's mother had returned home from work. She was surprised to find Anubhav still sitting there. At the same time, she felt happy too. A slender hope that had sprouted in her heart in the afternoon grew a little more. Ashim could see that his mother's pale face lit up after a long time. He liked this light reflected on her face. At the same time, he was apprehensive about this hope—this light. Ashim noticed that at the hem of his mother's chador, she had tied a small knot. Ashim knew that in this knot she kept the meagre amount of money which she earned from her odd jobs. And with that little money, she somehow managed to run the household. Today, Ashim wished to value that money more than just a means to mitigate their hunger.

After having another cup of tea prepared by Ashim's mother, Anubhav left their house. Soon, a jubilant Ajoli too returned home, this time dancing like a butterfly. Ashim wished she would remain exuberant like that always.

Gradually darkness descended, but Ashim felt as if his heart had lit up like an earthen lamp.

But who has ignited this lamp, he wondered.

Anubhav sir?

Nirmal?

36

Mahendra master was standing on the veranda outside the classrooms. He was looking in the direction of the school gate when something caught his eye. *Ashim!*

Clutching books in his hand, the boy was entering through the school gate, albeit hesitantly. It seemed like the boy was feeling embarrassed.

It was true. Ashim had not attended school for several months. Moreover, he was fearful and ashamed lest his classmates already knew about his recent arrest by the police. So, with hesitant steps, Ashim walked into the school campus.

Suddenly, Mahendra master got out of his reverie. He rushed towards the teacher's common room, almost running. Jilmil, who was sitting there, was shocked.

'What happened, sir? Everything all right?'

'The idiot has returned!' Mahendra replied awkwardly.

'The idiot? Who?' asked Jilmil, taken aback at the senior teacher's behaviour.

'Ashim!' Mahendra replied without meeting her gaze.

Jilmil tried to read Mahendra master's face, then she got up from her chair to go to the veranda. On seeing her get up, Mahendra called after her, as if frightened, 'Don't go there. He . . . he might feel uncomfortable.'

Jilmil returned to her chair. She noticed that the man was extremely restless and couldn't even sit properly at one place!

After some time, Anubhav entered the common room. Immediately, Mahendra got up and approached him. Staring at Anubhav's face, he couldn't find any words to say to the young teacher. So, he just patted him lightly on the back before rushing out of the room.

Anubhav looked towards Jilmil questioningly.

Jilmil replied with a smile, 'Ashim has come to school again!'

37

After school was over, Anubhav noticed Nirmal hanging about outside the teacher's common room. He instantly understood that the boy wanted to meet him.

Anubhav came out of the common room and walked towards the boy. Seeing his teacher, Nirmal too walked up to him.

However, he just stood silently with his head bowed in front of his teacher. His lips were quivering. Anubhav could feel that Nirmal was feeling a plethora of emotions that had made him speechless. He understood what the boy wanted to say; he wanted to express his gratitude but couldn't find the right words.

'You know, Nirmal, all this was possible just because of you!' Saying this, Anubhav patted Nirmal on the back, just as Mahendra had done to him a little while ago.

It was true, Anubhav thought. Nirmal truly deserved this affection and all the acknowledgement.

38

Ashim had been going to school for a few days now. However, he could feel that his friends didn't accept him like before. Previously, some of them had started avoiding him when he started falling behind in class. But this time around, except for Nirmal, almost all his classmates avoided him completely. They shunned him. Perhaps they felt that he was bad company, especially after the incident with the police. Maybe their parents had told them not to talk to him. The only exception was Nirmal. *Didn't his parents give him such instructions to stay away from me? Is he disobeying his parents? Would his studies also not suffer if he sticks to my company?*

At times, Ashim felt that the time he spent at the school was exactly like the time he had spent at the police station that day. Just as he had waited eagerly for his father to come and release him, in the same way, he eagerly waited for the school bell to ring and rescue him. He missed his old school life. Earlier, he used to enjoy classes and the company of his friends. However, he felt relatively free in Anubhav sir's class. Looking up to his teacher gave him strength. Moreover, his classes were interesting and Anubhav sir often kept referring to the related and relevant concepts that Ashim had missed in the previous years. As a result of this method of connecting the dots, Ashim was able to make up for the academic losses that he had suffered over the past two years.

In fact, Anubhav sir explained mathematical concepts so beautifully that Ashim felt like delving deeper into these theories. The man also had his own ingenious style of teaching mathematics. While solving a problem, he would ask students about each step repetitively thereby making them solve the problem on their own. And though it took a relatively long time to solve one problem, but thanks to this approach, Ashim and his classmates could understand the maths behind that particular problem properly. Their self-confidence got a boost, too. In fact, solving this one problem conscientiously benefited the students more than ten problems that a teacher would have solved for them. And even if the students failed to solve a maths problem, Anubhav sir did not solve it *for* them. He encouraged them to brainstorm and discuss among themselves. For example, even now, he had not yet solved the third question regarding consecutive composite numbers, even after so many days. Though the children would request him, he'd just say, 'I also don't know the answer. I'm also still trying.'

So while Ashim was able to enjoy the maths class, he was finding it difficult to deal with his peers. As he had not focused on his studies over the past few years, he didn't know a lot of things. This year too, he had wasted three months completely. As a result, there were a lot of topics about which he knew nothing.

While returning from school one day, Ashim shared this challenge with Nirmal.

'Hmm,' said Nirmal, contemplating. 'Do one thing! Come to my house in the evening every day. I will try to help you with your studies. And then Anubhav sir can help you out with concepts which even I don't know.'

'Oh, no, no!' Ashim said awkwardly, rejecting the proposal.

'But why?' asked Nirmal, surprised.

'If I take up your time, you will lag behind,' muttered Ashim gloomily. 'You know, Nirmal—nobody else wants to be my friend except you.'

'What do you mean?' Nirmal asked.

'Don't your parents scold you for being friends with me?'

'No, they don't.'

'Mahendra sir?' he asked hesitantly.

'No.'

Ashim paused. 'So, he doesn't say anything to you? Rebuke you for not concentrating on your studies and wasting your time with me?'

Nirmal shrugged. 'No, nothing of that sort. In fact, whenever he meets me, he just tells me to study well. That's it.'

'Then?'

'What then?' Nirmal asked, confused.

'Doesn't Mahendra sir rebuke you for being friends with me? For sitting with me in class?' Ashim's throat choked as he spoke.

'No, Ashim, no, he doesn't,' replied Nirmal, softly.

39

There was one thing that became quite apparent to every teacher in the school. It was that whenever Ashim saw Mahendra sir in the distance, he changed his direction. On the other hand, if Mahendra sir saw Ashim, he too altered his way, picking up speed while tidying up his dhoti.

One day, however, as fate would have it, both came face to face because they were distracted and forgot to maintain their distance.

Upon suddenly being confronted with each other, both stood awkwardly, staring at each other for a while. Thereafter, turning to their left, in sharp angles, in the manner of the *baye mud* of NCC cadets in a parade, they turned their backs to each other and then, with rapid strides, retreated in the direction from which they had come. It was as if two ping-pong balls had deflected after hitting a wall.

40

Since the day that Ashim was detained by the police, there had been a dramatic transformation in his father's demeanour. Neither did the man now ask for money to support his drinking habit, nor did he beat Ashim for not going to work at the quarry. He just remained indifferent.

Ashim and his mother felt relieved by this.

However, his father didn't give up drinking. And he also didn't increase the amount of time he spent at home. His father's rapport with the family remained uneasy. Earlier, he used to call out to his son at least once in the day for money, but now that too had stopped.

Ashim was both happy and sad about this change in his father's behaviour.

Occasionally, Ashim became apprehensive with an unknown fear: From where was he getting the money for his alcohol now? Had he adopted some illegal means to finance his bad habit? Was he on some dangerous path? Was their home going to be sold off? Was it on a mortgage with some unscrupulous loan shark?

On the other hand, his mother was finding it difficult to manage the expenses of their household after Ashim quit the quarry. In spite of that, her face exuded happiness. But the fact that he couldn't contribute to the house bugged Ashim constantly.

On three occasions, Anubhav sir had voluntarily given his mother money, and somewhat forcibly too. And though his mother had accepted it, she had done it somewhat hesitantly. In fact, his mother had kept exact accounts in the hope that one day she would be able to repay him. But both Ashim and his mother understood that this wasn't a permanent way of managing their finances and that Ashim had to find an alternative very soon.

Ashim decided to talk to his teacher. He had to convey to Anubhav sir his concerns regarding his father too. And Anubhav sir was the only person who would understand his situation.

41

Through Nirmal, Anubhav kept himself updated on Ashim. And so, very soon, he learnt that Ashim's classmates were avoiding him and that the boy was hurt by this mass rejection. However, Anubhav knew that if he broached the matter in class, not only would Ashim feel embarrassed, but his classmates would be uncomfortable as well. After much thought, Anubhav felt that, with time, this matter would solve itself.

Instead, he decided to help Ashim with his studies. The boy had suffered significant losses in his academic life over the last two years and even more in the past several months. And also, it would be unfair to dump this on to Nirmal, who was also just a child.

After school one day, Anubhav called Ashim and presented a proposal: 'I will tutor you in the evenings for some days. See Ashim, the thing is, if you don't recover your losses now, the things you don't understand will just pile up. The situation will snowball and, once this happens, you will not feel good about coming to school. Plus, your midterm exams are round the corner.'

Ashim didn't object. Already, Anubhav sir had gone above and beyond of what was expected from a teacher. In fact, he needed to do this as, eventually, this would lessen his teacher's burden. Ashim calculated: he had the textbooks of the previous classes, and moreover, Ajoli was a junior too. He could discuss with her the class VIII curriculum. And Nirmal had offered to help him too. All Ashim had to do was keep in mind that nobody had anything to lose by helping him. But he also didn't want to be a burden to anyone. Especially his teacher, who had been lending him money.

'Sir, I want to do something.'

Anubhav understood what the boy was trying to say: Ashim wanted to work and earn a little money to run the house. *Perhaps he doesn't like borrowing money*, thought Anubhav. *What would he call this emotion of a teenager? Self-respect?* Whatever be its name, Anubhav didn't want to disrespect this emotion because these feelings and sentiments made one human and gave one the motivation to better one's lot in life. 'I'll arrange for something within a couple of days,' he reassured Ashim.

Ashim nodded. The conversation was over, but he didn't leave.

'Do you have something to tell me?' Anubhav asked, picking up on Ashim's behaviour.

'Um . . . my father . . .' he started, 'he continues to . . . um . . . drink just as before. But he doesn't take any money from me nowadays,' saying this, Ashim paused. Then as if talking to himself, he said, 'I wonder from where he's getting the money to drink.'

Ashim's question got Anubhav thinking. *Is Ashim's father doing something he should not be doing? Is it an indication that soon Ashim's family's sigh of relief will become a sigh of sorrow?*

Immersed in their own thoughts, the two didn't know that within a very short period everything will reveal itself.

42

The scene startled Anubhav. He was walking back home after school, and although it was afternoon, the sun's rays were still quite intense. It was an extremely hot day, and everyone was parched. Anubhav was very tired too, and so he decided to walk slowly under the shadows of the rows of coconut palms that flanked the road.

Suddenly, he heard a piercing sound. It seemed like someone was clearing the weeds and overgrowth in the enclosed front yard of a house. It sounded as if the worker's hoe had landed on a broken glass bottle lying concealed in the ground, which shattered, giving off that awful sound. Intrigued, Anubhav peeped into the yard only to receive the shock of his life: It was Ashim's father, hoe in hand, sweating under the blistering sun.

It was as if a cool breeze soothed Anubhav's heart, and he stopped walking. On noticing the schoolteacher, Ashim's father too came forward and stepped up to the bamboo fence. The man didn't say anything, not even a word in greeting. But Anubhav knew that the man was naturally reticent and not expressive. On the previous two occasions as well, when they had met, the man hadn't uttered a single word. Yet, on both occasions, he himself had come to meet Anubhav.

Anubhav observed him intently: due to the excessive labour, the man was taking quick, shallow breaths out of exhaustion and drops of sweat were dripping from his body to the ground. His face had turned extremely red in the heat. It seemed like Ashim's father had been doing this for some time now. Anubhav could understand how much toil it required to work a hoe. *Could he provide a piece of fish to Ashim and Ajoli with the money earned through such intense hard work? Could he buy them notebooks for school? Could he gift his wife a new mekhela chador? Of course, he could but he wouldn't. All the money earned through his back-breaking hard work would be wasted on alcohol.* Anubhav sighed, thinking. *What makes this person waste all his hard-earned money on such a vile habit while his family continues to go hungry? Of course, the answer to this question does not lie in the word 'drunkard'.* Anubhav felt compassion for the man.

Wiping off the sweat on his forehead, the man said shyly, 'Working here on a daily wage . . .'

Anubhav nodded and tried to sound enthusiastic. 'Very good; that's very good. After all, the expenses for Ashim and Ajoli's studies have increased.'

Hearing this, Ashim's father got embarrassed and bowed his head in shame.

But Anubhav didn't stop. 'And, of course, you have to spend a lot on their clothing and other necessities too—I totally understand.'

This time, the man shook his head slightly.

'And then, Ashim's mother! You have to give her at least one new mekhela chador on Bihu or Puja, don't you?'

The man shook his head again.

But Anubhav didn't stop. 'You know, Ajoli's face has become too pale nowadays. She may be suffering from anaemia. Perhaps you could include a piece of fish for her lunch or dinner.'

The man writhed in a sort of uneasiness and started shaking his head vehemently.

43

Whenever Ashim visited Anubhav sir, his heart was overwhelmed with an inexplicable feeling. All the shelves and almirahs in each of the rooms were packed with books. There were books everywhere, even on the bed and on chairs. *Perhaps it was the same back home in Anubhav sir's hometown too,* reckoned Ashim. The books lent a certain gravitas to the rented house, and whenever Ashim entered it, he felt as if he were walking into a library.

When he visited Anubhav sir's house for the first time, he was awestruck! 'Wow! So many books!' he had said, looking around, spellbound.

Anubhav sir had just laughed and said to him in good humour, 'You know, buying books is not a heroic feat.'

After seeking Anubhav sir's permission, Ashim had taken a look at the books, moving from one stack and shelf to the next. For the first time in his life, Ashim found out there could be books on such diverse subjects!

From poetry, short stories, novels, general knowledge, philosophy to sports, there was nothing that wasn't part of Anubhav sir's book collection!

Observing Ashim's wonder, the teacher remarked, 'Jack of all trades!'

Not only books, Anubhav sir also had a large collection of CDs of Assamese songs. From old Assamese movie songs to the songs of 'Geetikabi' Pārvati Prasad Barua, 'Baulikabi' Kamalananda Bhattacharyya, 'Kalaguru' Bishnu Prasad Rabha and 'Rupkonwar' Jyoti Prasad Agarwala, the collection was vast and tasteful and Ashim had felt an intense urge to listen to those as well.

'Your subconscious self is formed by the kinds of books you read and the songs you listen to,' Anubhav had commented. 'Wherever you live and whatever you do in future, your subconscious self will determine the honesty and sincerity with which you dispense of your duties. How you accept your life and how you accept the challenges of life—everything depends on the resources inside your mind. Listening to music or reading books outside of your curriculum—these are not just means of relaxation to be enjoyed in your leisure time, Ashim. Most songs that are popular nowadays lack significance or depth of thought, I feel. These songs serve the immediate purpose of entertainment and don't enrich our minds. But when I listen to the songs of Jyoti Prasad Agarwala, Pārbati Prasad Barua or Jyotish Bhattacharyya, I am transferred into a different realm.'

Ashim had listened to his teacher's words with bated breath.

After thinking for a while, Anubhav sir had spoken again. 'Maybe you're finding it difficult to understand all these things right now. Yet, I feel I should talk about them with you. Otherwise, who else will discuss such issues with you? And when? What I am trying to say is that our attitude towards everything is mostly superficial. We don't delve deeply into issues. The modern world has made us all hollow on the inside. We love to make merry and have fun all the time, and we reckon that is what living a good life is all about. But that is not true. Had it been like that, a cheerful, fun-loving boy who loved to sing and entertain people would not have died by suicide,' he said softly, thinking about the boy Jilmil had spoken about previously.

'Remember, if a fun-loving, cheerful boy dies like that or does something harmful to others or engages in a drunken brawl somewhere, then there must be emptiness inside his mind, isn't it? Your mind is just like a bag. It is entirely up to you whether you want to fill it with garbage or with something beautiful. Just as the famous litterateur Bhabendra Nath Saikia once said, "You will make merry, you will make mischief, you will engage in quarrels. But amid all that, never forget one thing—you have to be a virtuous person." Yes, you have to always remember that, Ashim. You have to be a good person, a righteous man who can contribute meaningfully to society. You must not get bogged down by the troubles and sorrows of life. You have to keep on fighting, just like the players of a football team do when they are down by a couple of goals. And remember, you have to keep on striving to do so, but within ethical bounds and the legal framework. You have to be your own referee in this football match called life. In order to live your life in a meaningful way, you have to be like a sportsperson. At the same time, you have to keep your inner child alive. Full of wonder and innocence.'

Anubhav had then directed Ashim to a bookshelf. It was packed with books for children and teenagers. Ashim had started reading the names of the books from one end—*Tomalokar Val Houk (May You Receive Only the Good); Mohadustor Dusto Buddhi (The Antics of the Mischievous); Akhoror Jokhola (The Ladder of Letters); Moruwa Phul (The Marjoram Flower); Totto-Chan: The Little Girl at the Window; Little Prince; Shiskin, the Others, and I; Pinocchio; Gulliver's Travels; Shanto, Shisto Hristo Pusto Mohadusto (The Reserved, the Robust and the Ragamuffin); Alice's Adventures in Wonderland* . . . the list went on.

'Who reads these books for children, sir?' asked Ashim, curiously.

'I do! Why do you ask?' responded Anubhav, smiling. 'Nirmal and you can borrow and read these books too, if you guys want to. But there is one condition.'

'What condition?' queried Ashim.

'You have to handle these books with fondness and care.'

44

Anubhav had just entered the kitchen to cook when he heard someone banging on the door. As if on cue, the electricity went off and darkness descended. Taking out the mobile phone from his pocket, he turned on the torch and came out to the veranda.

It was Ashim's father.

'Take this!' he said, lifting a Roú fish, a popular freshwater carp, weighing almost one kilogram. The fish was as fresh as it could be!

Anubhav was amused. 'Arre! What will I, a single man, do with this huge fish? Better you take it home.'

'I . . . I feel embarrassed.' Saying this, the man placed the fish on the veranda.

'What?' Anubhav was surprised.

'Well, for the last three years, I have not taken anything home, be it rice, lentils, fish or meat. I have not even given a tattered garment to clothe Ashim, Ajoli or my wife. Their mother manages the expenses of their

studies and runs the household as well. And look at me—
I have not done anything for them! Even if I were to die,
it would not change anything for them.' Uttering these
words, the man stepped off the veranda and disappeared
into the darkness.

45

At last, an alternate means for Ashim to earn a living was picked out!

There was no newspaper agency in their village. So, Anubhav contacted the offices of the three most popular newspaper publications in the closest town and helped Ashim open a newspaper agency in the village. A little further from their village, an operational newspaper agency already existed—newspaper offices, through mutual agreement, sent all the newspapers in a single vehicle to that particular village. Now, newspapers for Ashim's agency too would arrive in that same vehicle. The plan was the van would make a little detour to Ashim's village and drop off the bundles of newspapers just outside his courtyard. Ashim would then get these delivered in his village.

After this, a goal was set—to acquire customers for Ashim's agency. So, all the teachers of Ashim's school, including a number of teachers in the primary school in the village, and several other elders agreed to buy newspapers from Ashim. All together, thirty customers were confirmed. Anubhav had done the calculation—if the distribution would yield a 35 per cent commission, then the monthly profit from thirty newspapers wouldn't be that meager. And this was just the beginning! If Ashim could do the job well, the number of customers would surely increase by word-of-mouth publicity. Then, he could even branch out into magazines and other periodicals, which could fetch more money.

Further, to set up a newspaper agency and to run it smoothly, not much capital was required. Nor was there any need for taking a room on rent in the village bazaar. As soon as the newspaper stacks arrived, Ashim would have them immediately distributed from house to house. So, there was no need to rent a warehouse or maintain an inventory. And after the end of each month, the due payment could be collected directly from the customers. However, another job needed to be accomplished—monthly bills of all three publications had to be deposited in the respective offices located in the city. Anubhav decided he would take Ashim with him a couple of times and show him how it was done, and thereafter, Ashim would be able to do it on his own.

However, one important question remained: how would Ashim distribute the newspapers? It was not physically possible to carry all the bundles and distribute them, door to door, on foot. Besides, when the number of customers would eventually increase, the burden to distribute the newspapers would increase too. At this rate, a better part of Ashim's day would be spent walking up and down the village leaving him little time to do anything else.

So after much thought, Anubhav decided to buy Ashim a bicycle. This was not charity as Ashim would repay him, little by little, by means of monthly installments from his earnings. This would make the boy feel more accomplished without weighing him down with the burden of receiving an expensive gift like a bicycle.

Once all the details had been finalized, it was Ashim's mother who made a request to Anubhav: 'It would be better to start the work on an auspicious date suggested by a priest.'

However, Anubhav rejected the proposal instantly. 'There's no need for that! What if we have to wait for one week or one month for the auspicious date to arrive? The day on which an honest work is begun automatically becomes an auspicious day, doesn't it?' he asked.

46

Ashim had developed a liking for his new occupation. The newspaper van usually arrived at 5 a.m. and the driver threw the bundles of newspapers outside their courtyard. Ashim was already up by then and raring to go! He lost no time in putting the bundles of newspaper into the bicycle carrier, riding out into the village immediately.

Going from house to house, Ashim would stop his bicycle in front of each customer's place for a moment and then throw the newspaper into the courtyard. Thereafter, ringing the bicycle bell a couple of times, indicating that the paper had arrived, he would pedal away. There was, however, an exception to this routine in case of two households. Ashim couldn't think of these two people simply as customers. First, Ashim never threw the newspaper into Nirmal's house. Every morning, he made it a point to deliver the newspaper to Nirmal by hand. And on the other side, his best friend too would wait eagerly for him. Next was Anubhav sir. The teacher too waited for Ashim with the same enthusiasm. For him, Ashim himself was a piece of wholesome and pleasant news. And every morning, Anubhav looked forward to those good tidings—day after day.

However, unbeknownst to Ashim, every morning at that particular time another person kept a watch over his gateway from a small opening in the window of his room. But that man never came out to the veranda to greet him—it was Mahendra sir!

He couldn't gather the courage to come out into the courtyard and greet Ashim. On the other hand, Ashim too would throw the newspaper hurriedly and leave the spot. He even didn't ring his bicycle bell!

But from behind the window curtain, Mahendra master would watch stealthily a boy's relentless struggle to excel in life.

47

The results of the boys' mid-term exams were out. As expected, Nirmal's performance was very good, and his results raised the expectations for his performance in the forthcoming matriculation exam.

Ashim's results were better than his results in last year's annual exam. He had scored more in mathematics than any other subject. Ashim was satisfied with his result. Yes, he was quite pleased with himself. He had returned to school again, resumed his studies and appeared in the exams. And now, he had passed in all the subjects—that too after studying for only two and a half months! So, whatever the outcome was, it was good.

But Nirmal was not satisfied. He called Ashim aside and started interrogating him, 'How did you perform?'

'I did well,' Ashim responded.

'What did you do well in?' Nirmal asked his best friend angrily.

'Well, I passed in all the subjects.'

'And?'

'I scored better in all subjects when compared to the previous annual exam!'

'So, you think that you've fared very well?'

'It's okay,' Ashim replied. 'I have been coming to school for less than three months, so this seems fine to me.'

'How much did you get in maths?'

'Sixty!'

'Why did you get *only* sixty?' he questioned his friend angrily. 'I'll punch you!'

'Wait!' Ashim smiled. 'Punching won't increase my marks overnight!'

'How is it that the boy who solved the maths problems which we all couldn't, could scrape by with just sixty marks?'

'Can't you see? I have been going through the previous years' concepts for the last few months.'

'Have you cleared all your doubts by now?' Nirmal inquired.

'Maybe,' Ashim replied, a bit uncertain.

'You've got to study properly for the pre-board test.'

Hearing this, Ashim's lost his patience. 'Wait, wait! Stop lecturing me. Tell me, how did you perform?'

'I fared well!' Nirmal replied in a content voice.

'How did you do well?'

'I scored better marks in each subject, you see.'

'So, you think you've performed well?'

'I think I did okay, if I say so myself.'

'How much did you score in maths?'

'Ninety-eight.'

'Why did you get only ninety-eight?'

Nirmal was quiet for a second and then burst into laughter. Ashim joined in too! After a while, Nirmal became serious. 'I was just kidding, Ashim. Actually, I am feeling very good today.'

Ashim too became somber. He was able to understand what Nirmal was trying to say.

'I am glad that you have done very well compared to your last academic performance,' said Nirmal, 'and that too, after just studying for only two and a half months. But you have to perform much better than this, you know. You have to do better than me. I am waiting for the moment when you become the topper again!'

Ashim started to feel a little uncomfortable now. He adored his friend and was also quite elated by Nirmal's excellent performance in the exam. It also meant that Ashim's company had not ruined Nirmal.

'You can do it, Ashim!' said Nirmal with great belief.

Nirmal's faith boosted Ashim's self-confidence. He was touched. 'You have a beautiful heart, my friend.'

'Have you seen my heart?' chuckled Nirmal. 'My heart is not at all beautiful!'

Ashim started laughing at Nirmal's words.

'Yes, I am speaking the truth! My heart is not beautiful at all!' said Nirmal with a smile. This time Ashim started laughing even more loudly.

Nirmal sighed and unbuttoned the two uppermost buttons of his shirt and lowered his vest a little. Ashim was shocked to see a thick surgery scar, about eight inches long, bang in the middle of Nirmal's chest. His mind became restless. Overcome by emotion, he felt like hugging his friend tightly.

But Ashim couldn't do it. He could only look at Nirmal, who had a dim smile still plastered on his face.

'Your heart is much more beautiful than I had thought,' said Ashim.

48

When Anubhav came to know about the surgery stitch on Nirmal's chest from Ashim, he felt sorry for the boy. Anubhav realized that Nirmal had undergone major heart surgery while he was still very young. Perhaps Nirmal had some congenital heart disease.

Anubhav's thoughts turned to Nirmal. He liked the boy very much; not only was Nirmal good in his studies, he was also a good person. He was not selfish or egotistical like some of the other bright students. And though Anubhav had started to help Ashim only recently, it was Nirmal who had been persistently trying to bring Ashim back to school.

Anubhav was amazed by the generous nature of the boy in spite of his serious health issues. He was proud of Nirmal because he had neither fallen into despair despite his misfortunes nor had he let Ashim forfeit his dreams. It was really unbelievable and quite commendable how Nirmal had been fighting silently against his adversities.

It is rare to find a boy like Nirmal—so righteous, brave and pure at heart, thought Anubhav. His heart was filled with admiration for the boy. Thinking about the two, Anubhav felt pride at the way the two had tackled the struggles of their lives and had developed such a deep sense of friendship. It filled him with a sense of inexplicable contentment.

Anubhav now recalled the night of Ashim's arrest. It was Nirmal who had informed him about what had happened. Later, Nirmal's father said regretfully, 'Actually, I too should've accompanied you . . .'

Anubhav realized the significance of that utterance today.

Nirmal's father hadn't completed the sentence. And at that time too, Anubhav had sensed something amiss in his incomplete words. But he hadn't pressed for more information. Anubhav realized now that, along with Nirmal, his parents too were fighting against this misfortune that their son was going through. Perhaps this hardship and this fight had made them kinder people and had imparted a measure of generosity in them. There was an undercurrent of sorrow in their lives; that much was true. But their kindness and compassion outshone their grief.

Nirmal's parents are lucky to have Nirmal as their son, thought Anubhav. *And I am lucky to have Nirmal as my student.*

49

It was Ashim's great fortune to have Nirmal as his best friend. Every morning when he handed over the newspaper to Nirmal, Ashim experienced that touch of great fortune from him. After this routine meeting every morning, Ashim would feel exuberant and he remained so for the entirety of the day!

Every morning, his determination to study well, to do good things and, more importantly, to become a good human being became more resolute. He had to do this for Nirmal's sake. Yes, he would *have to* become a good human being who could contribute positively to society. Yes, he was confident that he would be able to do achieve this. Nirmal's faith in Ashim gave him courage and a resolute conviction to be his best self.

50

From a modest thirty, the number of Ashim's customers soon increased to fifty. His earnings too naturally increased and he was able to repay all the money Anubhav sir had lent him. He had also been paying his teacher the cost of the bicycle in installments. This debt, too, was almost over, but for a couple of installments.

Ashim was even able to buy his mother and Ajoli two brand-new sets of clothes. When he gave his mother the mekhela chador with his first earnings, she wept profusely. Of course, she wasn't sad. These, Ashim assumed, were 'tears of pride and joy', as the adage goes. Ashim disliked this quirk of his mother; she would invariably shed tears be it for sorrow or joy! This was all so confusing at times for the young man.

Ajoli handled these emotions much better than her mother. She would cry aloud while rolling on the floor when she was upset and would flit around like a dragonfly when she was happy. When Ashim gave her the new dress, she started to skip around in excitement, as if it were the first instance in the whole wide world where a brother had gifted clothes to his sister! And the very next moment, after her frolicking was over, she started complaining how the dress was blue and not in her favourite red colour! She then promptly demanded a red dress from the income that Ashim would receive the very next month.

Ashim had laughed at her obstinacy. 'Let me return this and bring you a red one.'

'I like blue too!' she replied instantly.

'Only your name means innocence, but I know the true you!' Ashim had teased her.

'You know that it's not *my* fault, Dada. Maa and Deuta gave that name to me.'

Ashim had laughed and accepted his defeat! There was no winning with this girl!

However, when it came to his father, the problem of communication persisted. Ashim continued to be awkward around his father. His mother had urged him to gift a new shirt to his father. The one he currently wore was tattered and shabby. Of course, Ashim knew that. He bought a brand new shirt for his father. The question remained, though: who would give it to him? When he asked his mother, she replied, 'Can't you see I am not on speaking terms with your Deuta?'

When he asked Ajoli to give their father the shirt, she refused pointblank and zoomed away in the imaginary car that she was driving. So, Ashim was left with no option but to give the shirt to his father himself.

He saw his father sitting on the veranda. The man was dozing, with his head resting on his knees. Ashim could smell the foul odour of liquor wafting from him. After Ashim called out to his father a couple of times, the man responded without raising his head. 'Huh?'

'Take this,' said Ashim, holding out a package.

His father took the package in a half-awake state. 'Wh–what is this?' he slurred as if still in a drunken stupor.

Ashim didn't respond.

Opening up the package, his father was startled. 'For whom is this?' he asked, shocked at discovering the new shirt inside.

'For you.'

Ashim observed that his father's eyes were now wide open and it was as if he wished to wake up from his long slumber.

51

Anubhav was feeling a little uncomfortable. Whenever Jilmil found him alone in the teachers' common room, she would become unusually cheerful. Like today. School was already over, and the teachers had started leaving for home. On finding himself suddenly alone with Jilmil, Anubhav rushed to leave the staffroom. But before he could leave, she called out to him.

'Ashim has made noticeable progress, hasn't he?'

'Yes, he has.'

'But you know what?' Jilmil said in a serious tone.

Anubhav had no choice but to respond, 'What?'

'You are helping only one Ashim,' she remarked. 'There are thousands of such Ashims in our country. The progress of one such Ashim won't change our society or, for that matter, the country,' Jilmil declared in a straightforward manner.

'Hmm . . .' muttered Anubhav as he sat back in his chair in a reflective mood.

Yes, it was true in a way. Anubhav was helping only one Ashim.

In fact, he had not thought much about this whole thing, how his actions would benefit society or the country. For him, it was simple: He had come across a devastated teenager, a student, and as a human being and a teacher, he had encouraged the boy and helped him. It was a spontaneous emotional reaction.

After pausing for a while, Anubhav chose his words carefully before speaking. 'Yes, I'm helping only one Ashim. Actually, the incident itself, in which I met Ashim, was so sudden. As you just said, there are lakhs of children like him in this country. But if you view the issue through this lens, the question becomes abstract. For example, the Ashim whom I had met would be lost in a maze of statistics or in an abstract idea about the poor, the downtrodden or the exploited. When these things become abstract, the responses too become mechanical. Everything becomes a statistic. People can put forward lots of theories to explain the cause of misery. But the human cost gets brushed under the carpet. Political parties and other stakeholders get detached, and hence their efforts are less meaningful and effective. People like Ashim get dehumanized, and that's the greatest tragedy,' concluded Anubhav.

'Still, you can't discard socio-economic theories straightaway,' Jilmil reminded Anubhav.

'Yes, definitely,' he said. 'A renowned literary critic once said, "A theory is like a torch that lights up the road, but it is not the road itself." So is the case with political

and socio-economic theories. We have to move forward
by illuminating the roads. Instead of doing that, if we
flash the torch directly at the people, they will be blinded
and directionless. So, we have to calibrate our torches in
such a way that our society can be shown the right way.'

Jilmil thought for a second. 'You have found a
way out for one Ashim—you have helped him open a
newspaper agency. What if fifty more Ashims were to
seek your help?'

Anubhav smiled and added, 'I can't deny your
reasoning, Jilmil. If it came to making provisions for fifty
boys, the problem would reach a stage that would be
beyond what an individual could handle. If the number
increased exponentially to lakhs of children, extensive
and widespread public awareness and involvement would
be required for sure. Political parties, social welfare
organizations and governments would have to step up
and their ideologies would come under the scanner.
And we, as human beings, is it not necessary for us to
respond to what is happening before our eyes with a
sense of compassion?'

The atmosphere had turned serious now. So, Anubhav
continued, smiling, 'Well, I'm going to tell you a story,
so listen carefully.'

'Story?' Jilmil was surprised.

'Life is nothing but a maze of problems if one doesn't
pepper it with a few stories once in a while!' said Anubhav,
trying to sound philosophical.

Jilmil's eyes shone as she smiled.

Anubhav started narrating:

'One morning, a man went for a stroll on the beach. He saw thousands of starfish that had been washed ashore by the tide. The morning sun had started to shine brightly by now. The man understood that these sea creatures would die of heat if they lay there through the day. So, he picked up a starfish lying in the sand and threw it back into the sea. Thereafter, he threw another. Then another. In this way, he continued throwing the creatures back into the water. On seeing him, a passer-by inquired, "What are you doing? There are thousands of starfish lying here. What difference will it make if you save a few?" The man didn't reply. Picking up another starfish, he threw it into the sea. "But it will make a big difference to this small creature."'

Anubhav paused.

'Finished your story?' Jilmil asked Anubhav.

'Yup,' Anubhav replied.

'Listen then, I'm adding something to this story.' Without waiting for Anubhav's reply, Jilmil continued, 'Thereafter, the other person too picked up a starfish and threw it into the sea.'

It was as if Jilmil was not adding to the story but challenging Anubhav with a riddle. Jilmil's eyes sparkled with a tinge of mischievousness.

Anubhav—blushing as red as a ripe tomato—turned away to hide his embarrassment.

52

Ashim alighted from his bicycle. Taking the three newspapers intended for Anubhav sir, he opened the gate and walked in. He saw that his teacher was sitting on the veranda and reading a book. On catching sight of Ashim, Anubhav put down his book.

After handing over the newspapers to Anubhav, Ashim picked up the book that was lying on the table. He read the title, *The Little Prince*. Easy enough, but he found the author's name a bit weird.

'What a strange name!' he commented.

'Oh that . . . the author of this book is French. His name—Antoine de Saint-Exupery—is pronounced "Ahn-twan-duh San-teg-zy-pey-ree". He was an aviator. You know, Ashim, I've lost count of how many times I have read this book. Often, when I feel sad, I read *The Little Prince*.'

'Oh,' said Ashim. 'Then today you must be feeling sad?'

Anubhav smiled. 'Since I've got a mind, it tends to become sad at times.'

Ashim understood that Anubhav sir was skirting the issue. But he felt a tremendous urge to know why his teacher was feeling gloomy today. However, he was too shy to ask him directly.

'Sir, that mathematical problem you had assigned to the class—to cite examples of twenty consecutive composite numbers . . .'

Anubhav sat up, eager to know what Ashim's answer was.

'Oh yes, have you been able to arrive at the answer?'

'Perhaps.'

'Well then, tell me!' urged Anubhav, excited.

'Sir, the first number will be the one which we will get after multiplying the numbers from 2 to 21 and then adding 2 to the product, that is:

$2 \times 3 \times 4 \times 5 \ldots \times 21 + 2$

The second number will be:

$2 \times 3 \times 4 \times 5 \ldots \times 21 + 3$

And, the twentieth number will be:

$2 \times 3 \times 4 \times 5 \ldots \times 21 + 21$

'Well, so the numbers are consecutive. But are they composite?' Anubhav asked just to test Ashim. However, he was sure that Ashim would be able to explain it properly.

'Sir, the first number will be divisible by 2, the second by 3, and in that manner, the twentieth number will be divisible by 21. As such, each number will be composite.'

Anubhav was amazed!

'You know, you've lifted my mood!' exclaimed Anubhav, smiling.

Ashim was surprised too! *Can a teacher's gloominess vanish when their student solves a mathematical problem?*

Astonished, Ashim kept gazing at Anubhav's face. And so did the latter.

53

It was the second day of the school week, and something exciting was taking place.

An extempore speech competition was being held! Topics relating to various subjects had been written down on small strips of papers which were then folded and kept in a basket. Each student had to then pick up one chit and deliver a speech on the topic he or she found written on the paper.

Nirmal's topic was 'Lachit Borphukan', the famous Ahom military general. Quite naturally, the boy referenced the battle of Sharaighat, speaking about the valour of the great Assamese general who had thwarted Mughal invasion into the region. Nirmal also mentioned the incident where Borphukan had beheaded his own maternal uncle for the latter's half-hearted efforts during the battle, declaring, 'Nobody is greater than the nation, even one's own maternal uncle!'

However, it took only two minutes for Nirmal to cover all this. Every child was allotted five minutes! But Nirmal couldn't find anything more to say. He started feeling restless and experienced a degree of stage fright. Not being able to complete even five minutes, he was mortified. He kept standing on the podium, looking downcast. Soon enough, tears started rolling down his cheeks. Nirmal was immensely ashamed. After all, the great general Lachit Borphukan was the pride of Assam, and he hadn't been able to do justice to this state hero!

However, none of the teachers could scold or fault the boy. After all, they too knew hardly anything other than what Nirmal had already said!

On seeing Nirmal in such a state, Anubhav consoled him, 'It is not your or any other student's fault. After all, sufficient research on our glorious past is yet to be done in a meaningful way. And whatever little is known is not properly presented in the curriculum. History doesn't necessarily mean only wars or battles or, for that matter, a mishmash of uninteresting facts and dates! Be it teachers or parents, none among us encourage students to learn about things beyond the curriculum. Now look at us; we leave no opportunity to take pride in the fact that we belong to the land of Lachit. But how much do we really know about the general? Even his famous statement, "Nobody is greater than the nation . . ." is a figment of our imagination! Did you know, according to some historians, Lachit didn't really behead his uncle? But a mou-mai. In the Tai-Ahom language, mou-mai means an engineer who constructs earthworks or fortifications.

So, that means Lachit must have beheaded one such engineer or mou-mai, who could have been engaged in building the fortifications against the Mughals, and not his actual Momai or maternal uncle.'

Anubhav suggested that Nirmal read the book *Lachit Borphukan* by Surjya Kumar Bhuyan. 'You will find out many more facts relating to the history of Assam there and in the book *Asom Buronjir Kotha,'* he said, adding, 'if you want, I could bring both books for you.'

Having heard this, Jilmil made two requests to Headmaster Sanatan: Firstly, to give substantial books as awards to the students during the school week and, secondly, to build a well-stocked library in the school. 'For this, even if a nominal fee is collected from the students, a substantial amount of money can be accumulated,' she said. 'Teachers should also donate generously,' she suggested. Jilmil then proposed that Anubhav should be entrusted with the task of building the library with proper planning because 'only a bookworm should be in charge of a library,' she quipped, smiling.

The headmaster instantly agreed to all the proposals! 'Yes, this must be done as soon as possible,' he concurred.

*

As Ashim proceeded to climb up to the podium, he could feel all the eyes of the audience on him. Everybody was curious about Ashim already. Besides his eventful school life, the boy had been caught by the police! Suffice to say, he was a mystery to everyone. Moreover, after returning to school, he had made remarkable progress in just a few months.

Ashim gingerly chose a chit from the basket and read the topic to himself. His lips trembled. He tried to say something. But nothing came out of his mouth. His mouth had gone dry. He glanced around the hall, once at Nirmal and then at Anubhav sir. Everyone noticed as he blinked repeatedly as if something had entered his eyes. As Ashim stood there, mute, the headmaster was intrigued. He wanted to know what the topic was!

Ashim tried again. But again, his lips trembled. This time too, no words came out. Yet, he didn't descend from the podium.

Anubhav decided to intervene now, worried. Walking up to the podium, he took the paper from Ashim. 'The topic is—your favourite person!' Anubhav read from the chit. He looked at Ashim, overwhelmed by a sudden rush of emotions. The boy was frozen still. It was evident that he was trying hard to hold back an intense urge to weep.

Anubhav gently patted Ashim's head, and just at that moment, everyone noticed the dam of tears break suddenly and roll down the boy's cheeks.

54

Taking the newspaper from Ashim's hand, Nirmal asked him, 'Will you let me ride pillion on your bicycle to Anubhav sir's house?'

Surprised, Ashim asked him, 'This early? It's not even 6 a.m.!'

'Don't worry so much, Ashim. Let's go.'

'Have you sought permission from Khuri and Khura?'

'Yes. Of course, I've asked my parents.'

Ashim and Nirmal rode to Anubhav sir's house. Then, dropping him off, Ashim went on his regular route to distribute the rest of the newspapers.

Anubhav was surprised to see Nirmal at his house so early in the morning, but he tried not to show it.

'I'm sure you're surprised to see me at your house so early, sir,' Nirmal said, trying to muster a smile.

'No, no. What brings you here, Nirmal?'

Nirmal remained silent.

'C'mon in, let's have some tea,' offered Anubhav to put the boy at ease.

Inside, Anubhav made tea for both of them. Taking a sip from his cup, he asked Nirmal once again, 'What brings you here?'

Looking down at his cup, Nirmal mumbled, 'I was upset, so I thought of speaking to you.'

Anubhav felt a sudden jolt. His heart started to feel heavy.

'I have congenital heart disease, sir,' whispered Nirmal, 'and I underwent a major surgery sometime back.'

Anubhav didn't know what to say to comfort him. The house had gone silent.

'My heart is not like that of others, sir . . .' he said.

Anubhav gently took Nirmal's hand in his own. 'I'm aware . . .'

A few moments passed, and both remained silent.

'Are all the flowers in a garden the same, Nirmal?' said Anubhav, finally breaking the silence. 'Each flower has a beauty of its own. Your life too has a splendor of its own.'

'But does my life have any meaning, sir?' the boy asked sadly.

Anubhav felt heartbroken. The boy who was ever ready to help his friends, the boy who had saved Ashim from the brink of destruction—that same boy harboured such a deep wound inside his heart, a wound which he had concealed so very carefully.

'Why do you think that your life doesn't have any meaning, Nirmal?' asked Anubhav, uttering each word with a deep sense of affection. 'If you think about it in such a way, then whose life really has any meaning? Listen, I know that your life has a purpose. Ashim knows it, and so do your parents. But most importantly, you should know that. Your illness or suffering cannot render your life meaningless. Your life has meaning for the world around you and it has significance to you. You know about the physicist Stephen Hawking, right? When doctors shared with Hawking that he would only live for a couple of years, he could have given up, saying his life had lost all meaning or purpose. However, Hawking wrote that it was in that moment of his life when he finally understood its value. He started to enjoy his life from that moment on. And, trust me, this is not a fictional account meant to cheer you up. It really happened.'

Anubhav got up and brought out Stephen Hawking's *Black Holes and Baby Universe* from his bookshelf. Turning to a section in the book, he started reading, 'In fact, although there was a cloud hanging over my future, I found to my surprise that I was enjoying life in the present more than I had before.'

Anubhav paused and kept the book aside. 'It's my privilege that I have met you and can call you my student,' he said softly. 'It's Ashim's fortune to have found you as his supportive friend. For your parents, they are blessed to have you as their child and your achievements must fill them with joy. Your life is a great achievement for you as well. I understand there are sorrows and sufferings in your life. But in spite of all these battles, you have to win and surpass all the hurdles that life throws at you. And in order to achieve that, you have to be brave. Instil and nurture a fighting spirit within yourself. I know you went through a major surgery. But tell me, how many have a pure heart like yours? Just as your heart is different from others, so is your mind. You have to teach your mind courage and nurture a fighting spirit. Don't expect to hear kind words from each and everyone around you. And most importantly, don't get disheartened by the discouraging words of others.'

Glancing at Nirmal's face, Anubhav could see that the gloominess on his face was almost dissipated. Anubhav was relieved now. He smiled and said, 'Nirmal, sometimes things happen in your life which you can never anticipate. Not everything in your life unfolds according to your wishes or your best-laid plans. Pain and suffering are part of human life. It may be more for some and less for others. You cannot divide the amount of pain and suffering by measuring them with a weighing scale now, can you? So, there is no point in crying over why your share of pain is greater than others. Let me tell you something that I have told Ashim as well—accept life with a sporting spirit.'

'I can't help but feel sad and dispirited at times,' Nirmal said sadly.

'Well, it is only logical. Since you have a mind, you are bound to feel sad at times. But you must not store those sad feelings inside. Confide your feelings in a person who thinks like you and who understands and reciprocates your feelings. Talk to your friends and unburden your mind.'

'Sir, can I come to you when I feel sad?' Nirmal asked innocently.

The boy's earnestly spoken words touched Anubhav to the core. Be it Nirmal or Ashim, the boys regarded him as an ally. What more could he want?

Anubhav somehow managed to blurt out, 'Definitely.'

55

From the time Ashim started going to school again, he had lost contact with his peers at the stone quarry. In fact, he had not seen Ramen, Ratan and Dipak for a long time now. It was as if they were inhabitants of two parallel universes, detached from one other.

One day after school was over, Ashim decided to meet his former workmates. He went to the quarry at the foot of the hill. From a distance, he saw the boys with whom he had spent an important episode of his life. He felt sad for them. He felt as if they were rats caught in a trap. He too was caught till Nirmal and Anubhav sir rescued him. But these boys, they had no one who could free them.

Ashim slowly approached them.

Lifting their heads, they glanced at him once. Thereafter, they got back to smashing stones again. In his previous phase of life, if they had seen him approaching like this, they would have greeted him noisily and would have engaged in silly banter with him. Then, Ramen would have teased him with the word 'jewel' hurling filthy abuses at him. But today was different. They were silent and indifferent.

Ashim realized that they had already bid him adieu from their world. He could not infer what feelings they harboured for him now. He could only understand that he had been exiled. Did they think of him as a selfish person who had escaped at the first available opportunity, leaving them behind? That world was an extremely ruthless world. *Perhaps*, Ashim thought, *I had been searching for an escape route.* Had he visited Nirmal with the hope of finding escape routes? Did he cheat Ramen and his other mates?

Ashim felt very embarrassed. He could sense that Ramen and the others were also feeling uncomfortable with his presence. Disappointed, he turned to go back. Just then, he noticed Ramen getting up. He saw the boy throw his hammer on the stone heap and walk towards him. Ashim felt very happy. *Let Ramen tease me by calling me 'jewel'. Let him hurl abuses at me, call me names. Let him attack me with filthy words, after all, I deserted them.*

Ramen stopped in front of Ashim. Looking at him, he said, 'You've done the right thing, Ashim. Study well.'

The quarry came to a standstill.

Ashim sensed that the hammer blows in the foothill had stopped. Everyone was looking at their exchange. Ashim felt, as if on their behalf, Ramen had come forward to tell him what was on their minds.

Ashim looked at Ramen's face, were his eyes moist? Was he in pain?

This Ramen who used to taunt and tease him relentlessly, call him hateful words—was it the same boy standing in front of him? Did Ramen carry in his heart some goodwill for him? Did he have a soft corner for Ashim which had brought him to tears?

56

Anubhav was pleased when he heard that Ashim had visited his old companions at the mine. It showed that Ashim had not forgotten his old workmates.

Finding an opportunity one day, Anubhav brought up the matter in the teachers' common room. Everyone took interest in the topic, particularly Headmaster Sanatan and Mahendra master.

'There are some practical problems in bringing back those students who've dropped out of school long ago,' said the headmaster. 'There will be a big age difference between them and the regular students and that might be an impediment for both.'

'But students who dropped out of school some three or four years ago can be brought back from the next session in January. We first need to figure out their reasons for leaving,' suggested Mahendra master.

'Primarily, two reasons,' said Prashanta. 'Some lose interest in their studies. This could be due to their deteriorating performances in exams because of their failure to understand the curriculum.'

'So that means we teachers will have to teach this section of students with patience and compassion, and if needed, separately,' suggested the headmaster.

'Yes,' Prashanta continued. 'Second, there are others who drop out because they, simply put, cannot afford it. These students need special provisions. Their fees may be waived off. Moreover, with a little thought, one could come up with providing them a means of livelihood, as was done in the case of Ashim. Maybe a few of them can be engaged in Ashim's newspaper agency? As the number of customers increases, Ashim could benefit from some help in distribution, perhaps?'

There was a hum of agreement in the teachers' room. Everyone was excitedly discussing new ways to rehabilitate the lapsed students.

Then Jilmil proposed a plan, 'About three or four cultural nights are held in the village round the year, mainly during Bihu and Puja, right?' she said enthusiastically. 'Those cultural nights usually begin at midnight, and there, we see young artists shouting in the name of singing, with wrong pronunciation, improper acting and tuneless music.'

Everyone agreed, nodding.

'And as we all know,' she said, rolling her eyes, 'the majority of the spectators who remain till the end of these "cultural nights" are drunk to the hilt, creating a ruckus. It's shameful that several lakhs of rupees are spent on such shows. In my opinion, we should oppose this. Even if a

single cultural night is cancelled, money thus saved can
be used in creating a fund for poor students, isn't it?' she
asked, looking around.

But Prashanta sir expressed his reservation, saying that
the enthusiasm with which people donate generously
for a cultural programme might not be present for an
unglamorous charity drive like theirs.

Anubhav too felt the same. 'I agree with Prashanta sir
as our people are excited about two kinds of activities—
religious rituals and cultural nights.'

Annoyed, Jilmil retorted vehemently, 'C'mon! In
our village, there are several non–political organizations
which claim to think about and work for the welfare
of society. There is also a non-governmental Panchayat
which imposes fines to the tune of a thousand rupees
when a couple elopes! We should try, at least! We should
request everyone by saying, "Hey! The enthusiasm
with which you people collect donations for cultural
nights during Bihu, please show us an equal amount of
enthusiasm to collect donation, once a year for the school
and for the village library,"' she said, pausing.

Everyone became silent.

'This school is not the sole responsibility of the ten
teachers that work here,' she sighed. 'The village or for
that matter the nation will not progress just by celebrating
religious functions or cultural nights with much fanfare.
Unemployed youths riding motorbikes carelessly, listening
to noisy music, playing carom or cards by the side of the
road for hours on end, or doing the bidding of crafty
politicians—won't make a village progress. This village is

gradually becoming hollow from the inside. And it is up to us to keep an eye out and stop that from happening.'

Jilmil held forth for a while. While listening to her spirited lecture, Anubhav noticed her eyes; they looked like blazing fireballs, such was her passion.

57

It was the last day of the pre-boards. It meant that practically, it was the last day for the students of class X. After the exam was over, Nirmal came out to the school veranda with a heavy heart, looking for Ashim. He saw his best friend standing under the bakul tree.

'How was your exam?' asked Nirmal, walking up to Ashim.

'Better than the midterms. What about you?'

'Good,' shrugged Nirmal, pausing briefly. 'Um . . . Ashim, Mahendra master wants to meet you.'

'Why?' asked Ashim, taken aback.

A considerable amount of time had elapsed since that unfortunate incident, but Ashim still avoided his former teacher like the plague. Talking was out of the question; Ashim didn't even look in the direction of Mahendra master if he could help it. And to be fair, even the teacher avoided him.

'I don't know the reason,' shrugged Nirmal. 'But he said that he wants to meet you.'

'Okay. Let's go.'

'To meet Mahendra master?' Nirmal asked Ashim spiritedly.

'No. Let's go home!' replied Ashim unenthusiastically.

Nirmal found himself in a fix. He couldn't decide what he should do. Just then, he saw Mahendra master approaching them. His heart started pumping rapidly with anxiety.

Ashim too noticed the man coming towards them. 'Nirmal, I'm going; you stay here, okay?' Uttering these words, Ashim started to make a move.

'Wait. Please don't. I can't take the tension,' said Nirmal, clasping Ashim's hand.

By now, Mahendra master was near them. He glanced at Nirmal once. Thereafter, looking at Ashim, he asked, 'How was your exam?'

Ashim didn't respond.

Nervous, Nirmal pinched Ashim, urging him to reply. But still, the boy kept standing, looking in another direction.

To ward off the awkward silence, Nirmal replied, 'It was good, sir. Better than the mid-terms. But we expect the final one to be even better.'

Mahendra sir smiled. 'Yes, of course, it will definitely be good. Make sure you study hard,' he said.

Again, an awkward silence prevailed.

'Um . . . so I suppose you have decided to not talk to me for the rest of your life.'

This time too Ashim didn't reply. He just kept standing, staring at his feet.

Extremely embarrassed to be stuck between the two, Nirmal looked at Ashim through the corner of his eyes, conveying the message, 'Respond or else once Mahendra master leaves, I will give you a good scolding!'

'Will you remain offended with me forever?'

Ashim remained silent.

Disappointed, Mahendra master turned to leave, saying, 'Go home. Study well.'

Ashim remained silent.

And so, the once-awfully frightening teacher left them with a sad look on his face.

'Why didn't you reply, Ashim?' shouted Nirmal, irritated.

Ashim remained silent. He just kept looking at the ground.

'You don't even know that after that incident, Mahendra sir returned to our classroom with a bottle of Dettol and cotton to nurse your wounds?'

Shocked, Ashim raised his head.

'And you know what? I suspect, it was because of that incident and because of you that he gave up teaching our class.'

Conflicted, Ashim turned his head to look in the direction of Mahendra master's departing frame. Nirmal too looked in that direction. But by that time, the teacher had disappeared from their sight.

58

The temperature had dropped considerably in the village, and dew drops had started to accumulate on the surrounding vegetation. Perhaps because of that, Ashim woke up quite late on that particular morning. Freshening up quickly, he ran towards the gate. He was late for his deliveries!

Running to the gate at the edge of their courtyard, Ashim saw that the newspaper bundles were yet to arrive. He was surprised! *That's strange*, he thought. *Usually, the papers are delivered quite early. And till now, there has never been any delay in the arrival of the newspapers.*

Pacing frantically around the gateway, Ashim waited, but the newspapers never arrived. By now, Ashim had become quite stressed. *People become irritated when they don't get the paper on time,* he thought. *Did the vehicle break down somewhere enroute to our village? Was there a new driver who missed my house?* thought he. Nervous, Ashim stepped out on to the road to check.

But there was no sign of the bundles of newspapers anywhere.

To calm his nerves, Ashim brought out a book to read. But he couldn't concentrate. He thought that reading might calm his nerves, but it didn't help. Not even a little bit. Occasionally, he got up from the table and went to the gate to take a look. But the newspaper bundles never arrived. Gradually, the sun started to appear, piercing through the thick veil of fog. By this time, on other days, he would have been back home after distributing the newspapers. Ashim gave up hope now, terribly upset.

By now, Ajoli too had woken up and was at the study table, as was the norm. Her annual exams were round the corner. And not many days were left for Ashim's matriculation exams too. Usually, he too would have joined Ajoli after coming home from his rounds. But today, Ashim couldn't focus at all.

Tring! Tring!

Ashim heard the sound of a bicycle bell outside the house. He ran out.

It was his father! That too on his bicycle!

It was only then that Ashim noticed his bicycle was missing. It had not even been in the house! So even if the newspaper bundles had arrived on time, he would not have been able to go out to distribute them.

Irritated, Ashim asked, 'Where have you been so early, that too on the bicycle?'

'Ehh . . .' Ashim's father spoke hesitantly. 'I . . . I've distributed the papers today.' Then, as if everything was hunky-dory, he pushed the bicycle along and, perching it properly on its stand, walked inside.

Ashim stood there, frozen. It was as if a soft, heart-warming melody was slowly making its way into his heart. Composing himself, Ashim expressed his concern, acting as if all was normal. 'Do you know the customers? God knows to whom you have given which newspapers! I'll have to listen to their complaints tomorrow, you know.'

'No, no. I checked the names in the agency's account book. You had written the name of the newspaper against each subscriber's name. I've distributed the newspapers after looking at those entries,' saying this, he handed Ashim the account book.

Ashim stood here, his mouth agape.

'Let me distribute the papers from now on,' said his father. 'You should concentrate on your studies. Only a few days are left for your matriculation exams, isn't it?'

Speechless, Ashim entered the house. Throwing himself on his cot, he buried his face in the pillow.

Ajoli, who was studying nearby, observed that her elder brother's body shook occasionally.

59

One month back, Jilmil had promised her colleagues that she would show them a magic trick. And today was D-day!

Everyone noticed that Jilmil had placed a wooden box on the table. The box was familiar to all.

More than a month ago, the non-governmental Panchayat of the village adopted a resolution which stated that it would organize a three-day yajna for the well-being of the village. For that purpose, the Panchayat had planned to collect donations. Villagers were asked to contribute whatever they could depending on their financial situation. And for that purpose, a donation box had been maintained in the bazaar.

When Jilmil had come to know about this, she had made a proposal: that they too would ask for donations from the villagers to construct a library in the school and for their initiative to rehabilitate the school dropouts. And so, she too had kept a donation box in the village bazaar.

Jilmil got up from her seat and stood next to the box.

'Ladies and gentlemen!' she bowed. 'This is the donation box that we placed alongside the donation box for the yajna. We distributed leaflets urging people to donate generously. So far,' she paused, looking at everyone, 'as I have come to know, they have collected about Rs 1,50,000 from various places outside the village and from some traders in the city. And the villagers' contributions have been collected in their donation box. They opened their donation box yesterday. Around Rs 30,000 has been collected in that donation box. There are 800 families in our village. Therefore, on average, a contribution of Rs 25 has come from each family. Now, let's see what they have contributed to our cause.'

Two teachers stepped up to open the donation box. The money was counted. It was a little less than Rs 2000. All present in the teachers' common room fell silent. Like an expert magician, Jilmil gave a disarming smile and started speaking eloquently, 'Hope everyone has enjoyed my magic! The yajna organized for the well-being of our village attracted a total donation of Rs 30,000 from our village itself. About Rs 2,00,000 worth of donations were collected from both inside and outside the village. Now we will happily watch that money go up in flames! I don't know what good will come of it. But I guess the priests will benefit surely?'

Everyone remained silent.

'And our donation box was left in the market for an additional week!' she said mockingly. 'Well, at least, you might have noticed that there are three 500–rupee notes in our box. It means that at best three people have donated those three notes. Had those three people not been there, the situation would have been worse.'

Hearing Jilmil's words, Headmaster Sanatan cleared his throat and said, 'I had a strong premonition that such a thing would happen! Lest you get demoralized, I had put two 500-rupee notes in the box secretly!'

Everyone started laughing.

Anubhav's mind raced. *Who else might have contributed the remaining 500-rupee note? Nirmal's father?*

'Sir, you won't get these notes back!' declared Jilmil chirpily.

'Arre! And why should I take back the money? I will contribute another Rs 1000 instead! Just don't get dejected and continue steadfast on your mission,' said the headmaster with a smile.

'What if we do one thing?' offered Anubhav thoughtfully.

Everybody turned towards his voice.

'Let us approach the president, the secretary, as well as the members of the Panchayat and persuade them to give us a portion of their collection to establish a library. We could convince them that, by sharing their collection, they would be spending a portion of the amount on something tangible for our village. It will be a permanent asset for the entire community too.'

Jilmil spoke in a mock-serious tone, 'The proposal sounds good. But prior to that, we have to purchase a few cricket helmets, pads, gloves, thigh guards, arm guards, etc. with the money we have collected so far!'

'Why?' Anubhav asked, shocked.

'We have to make our delegates wear those before sending them off to the battlefield!' Jilmil quipped, laughing.

Everyone burst into laughter. Amid that laughter, everyone heard Jilmil's voice clearly, 'But let me promise you this. We will do it. We will not only establish the library but also bring the children back to school again. Our teachers have already decided to contribute for this noble cause. Now we will contribute even more handsomely. What we have decided, we will pursue with all our heart.'

Anubhav noticed that the face of this otherwise jubilant woman had suddenly become resolute with a sense of purpose.

This is also a kind of magic, thought Anubhav, smiling.

60

Anubhav was sitting in a corner in the teachers' common room, all alone. He was not feeling well mentally. A kind of despair had drained him, making him feel exhausted. By now, the teachers as well as the students had already left for the day. Anubhav kept sitting, too fatigued to get up from his chair.

Earlier in the day, the prize distribution ceremony had been observed at school. Along with that, their dream library, which had been built spiritedly by the teachers and the students together, had been finally unveiled.

A leading intellectual of the state had been invited as the special guest to inaugurate the library. That individual could be seen on prime-time television for at least five out of the seven days in a week! Anytime you'd turn on the TV and click on the local channels, you'd see him delivering eloquent speeches on various topics. Give him a topic, and he could speak on it for hours. However, this did not mean that all his views were worthy of prime-time

265

TV. Once, this man had said in a panel discussion that in ancient India, it was common practice to own beautiful girls and keep them as public property. Anubhav didn't know what research had gone into this so-called study. But whatever it was, it was disgusting, to say the least. On top of that, the man had the gall to state that the said custom was, in fact, scientific!

That day, when he had seen this debate, Anubhav got so tremendously angry that he couldn't even sleep properly. Then, recently this particular character had again said something insipid: He'd remarked on a popular social networking site that people who studied mathematics could not appreciate the bounty and beauty of nature. But that was not all of it. He'd gone on to say that since he didn't like mathematics, he wasn't obligated to keep a count of the money in his wallet and couldn't be bothered with how much he owed and to whom. He didn't even keep track of how much money he received as salary.

Seeing the post, Anubhav had wondered: *Is it not unbecoming of a person who happens to be the principal of a college and who identifies himself as an educationist, to make such frivolous public statements?* And it seemed Anubhav wasn't the only one he had put off. Irritated, one person commented on the post by adding in a sarcastic note, 'Since I dislike mathematics, I don't keep track of how much money I embezzle through my college! Since I dislike mathematics, I make frivolous statements!'

That such a person had been chosen to unveil their beloved library was precisely the reason why Anubhav was unhappy today. After all, a lot of their hopes were riding on the library that had been built with a lot of heartfelt emotions. A sort of unease was niggling at Anubhav's mind. He now mulled over the speech the man had made earlier today at the function.

In his one and a half hour-long lecture, this gentleman spoke about everything under the sun—free economy, globalization, capitalist education system, so on and so forth—and finally had happily declared that the current education system was of no use to society! He had gone on to say that, in fact, students didn't even need such education to gain employment. The existing schools and colleges were nothing but factories producing unemployed youths!

Anubhav was annoyed upon hearing this. His mind buzzed with questions and retorts: is securing a good job the sole objective of education? Doesn't education have any other objective? Is it proper to instil a sense of urgency to procure a job in the formative minds of the students of class VII, VIII or X? Shouldn't they just enjoy the process of learning? And also, what was the point of harassing the students by speaking about so many complex things for one and a half hours? Was it so important for a student of class VI to know the limitations of globalization? Did they even know what it meant?

The gist of this loquacious one-and-a-half-hour-long lecture was that students wouldn't get anywhere if they continued to study in the existing education system. Their future looked extremely bleak!

This had terrified Anubhav, as the speaker was practically an influential public figure. And it was natural for anyone to gravitate towards and believe famous people they saw on TV. *Is it proper to push these children into despair like this?* he wondered. *Listening to such discouraging notions repeatedly, won't they succumb and give up? What if they gave up studying altogether? Then, won't that despair get converted into unrest and delinquency?*

Anubhav was more upset, as the man had used the prize distribution ceremony to voice such stupid, personal and irresponsible opinions. He could tell that not only the students but also the teachers and parents alike were disheartened by the speech today. The lecture had no correlation with the spirit and vision with which the school's teachers spent their days working for the betterment of the students.

61

Anubhav heard footsteps approaching the teacher's lounge.

'What happened? Not going home?' Jilmil asked, entering the room.

'I'm upset,' Anubhav replied bluntly.

'What? Why?'

'Should the school's prize distribution ceremony be a platform for this so-called intellectual to disseminate his misinformation?'

Jilmil laughed.

'You know, I felt like saying just one thing to this man,' Anubhav fumed.

'What?'

'Tell us a date from which our society and our education system will become flawless. Let's all come to school from that day onwards. Till the time that much anticipated day arrives, please make arrangements to shut down all educational institutions.'

Seeing Anubhav fuming like this, Jilmil laughed. She was touched by his simplicity and the way he vented his anger. Jilmil often felt Anubhav's remarks were not always right, but at least they were pure and heartfelt.

Without letting her face betray her feelings, she remarked, 'You're a bit intolerant towards other people's ideological standpoints.'

'No, don't get me wrong,' replied Anubhav. 'Everyone is entitled to their ideological views. They can discuss their viewpoints and propagate the same. However, we cannot press the pause button on our lives until the moment a healthy, flawless society or education system comes into existence. Whatever the '–ism' or ideology, the discussion or the way it is spread or implemented, it should not harm our society at large, nor should it propel people into despair. Of course, we should think about the future and the progress of our civilization, but at the same time, we have to think about the present, about the joys and sorrows of our transient lives too, shouldn't we? Now, by this, I don't mean to say one should indulge in immoral enjoyment.'

Jilmil interrupted Anubhav, 'What are you getting at?'

'Well, you are aware of how much I love Nirmal, Ashim and the other students under my care. Do you know what saddens me whenever I meet Nirmal? That the pharmaceutical companies don't spend as much on the research for children's congenital heart disease as they do on, say, hair loss. It is because the return on investment is low there and it is not profit-making in the long run.

Isn't that a pity? And I'm not the one saying this; a lot of renowned cardiologists around the world are actually saying that paediatric cardiology is a much-neglected subject. It is because of such neglect that I feel for Nirmal. I feel guilty that I'm part of this so-called civilization that is so greedy, short-sighted and vain. Now, for this kind of non-profit research, the initiative must be taken by the government—the government run by a party with strong ideological standpoint. Governments that run like corporates won't take up such initiatives.' Anubhav sighed. 'I think I have spoken too much. Let's go as it's getting late,' he said, getting up from his chair.

Jilmil, too, stood up sombrely.

'You know, Jilmil, to be honest, I never liked this man.'

'Then why didn't you object when his name was proposed?' Jilmil retorted.

'This school doesn't belong to me alone, does it? Every one of you is a stakeholder here.'

'Hmm . . . you're right,' she replied. 'Well, even I don't have faith in him, if I am being completely honest.'

'And why is that?' asked Anubhav, intrigued.

Jilmil narrated an incident. A few years back, she appeared for an interview for the post of lecturer at the college where this man served as the principal. Jilmil had worn a shalwar kameez for the interview and not a mekhela chador, the attire traditionally worn by women in Assam. And before the conversation could even proceed, the man had made his displeasure evident. 'This is the first instance in the history of our college that a woman has appeared in an interview clad in shalwar kameez.'

'What?' Anubhav asked, shocked. 'How was he dressed?'

'In a three-piece suit, complete with neck tie, just like a perfect English gentleman would,' replied Jilmil.

'If he thinks that one should wear Assamese attire on all occasions, he himself should have led by example,' remarked Anubhav and continued sadly. 'I just don't know what to say.'

'Nah, our people want both tradition and modernity. And they thrust upon us womenfolk to uphold all traditions! Anyway, the duty of bringing in modernity rests on the shoulders of men, it seems,' Jilmil said in a sarcastic tone while a mischievous smile played on her face.

Anubhav thought, *Some people find mathematics hard. That's not a big issue. But a so-called intellectual who feels mathematics to be an unnecessary subject and holds the subject as well as the people connected to it in contempt is bound to make such frivolous, laughable statements.*

'He even wants to make girls he considers beautiful into public property!' The words slipped through Anubhav's mouth.

'What?' shouted Jilmil, enraged. 'Had he said that to me, I would have said, "I will hang a garland of slippers around your neck—you cheap person! How dare you say this to me!"' she said, crossly and rather loudly.

Terrified at her pitch, Anubhav looked around the room. He saw the school guard looking at them! It seemed he had walked in and heard only parts of their conversation. Looking at the man, Anubhav fumbled, 'She . . . she's not talking about me. I haven't said or done anything. It's that guest speaker . . . He's the one . . .'

62

The final exams were just around the corner. Ashim had more or less covered the entire syllabus. Looking back, he found it hard to believe how much he had missed in the last three years. However, he was satisfied with what he had been able to achieve in the short time since he had returned to school. He was happy that, in spite of all that had taken place, he had finally completed high school, which would culminate with his matriculation exams.

Since the board exams were due, class X students were required to stay home and study. So these days, all the students were at home. However, that did not mean that they didn't know what was happening in the school—good or bad. They'd already heard about the new library and how the melodious songs of Jyoti Prasad Agarwala, Bishnu Prasad Rabha, Parvati Prasad Barua, Kamalananda Bhattacharya and many others were also being preserved there. Even special arrangements had been made for students to listen to these valuable records.

They'd also come to know about a list that had been prepared, charting the names of those who had dropped out of the school in the last three years. Currently, the teachers were discussing how to bring these dropouts back into the fold.

The students of class X also got to know about the three-day cultural night programme that was going to take place in the village. The committee alleged that Anubhav sir, Jilmil ma'am and a few other teachers had conspired to stop this, and they had accused them of being uncultured. Ashim and his friends were quite amused, for they were familiar with these committee people! *Weren't these the same vagrants who often indulged in drunken brawls at the market square? How could these philistines assess the worth of Anubhav sir and Jilmil ma'am? In order to assess someone else's worth, shouldn't one have some value of their own to begin with?*

As Ashim mulled over this, he didn't know that an unfortunate incident would occur in the future, which no one could have anticipated.

63

It was quite evident that Anubhav had made a few enemies
in the village, especially in the cultural committee.
The young men there were particularly unhappy with
the maths teacher. Their main gripe was that Anubhav
was an outsider who didn't belong to the village. In their
language, he wasn't a 'local'. And, of course, according to
them, Anubhav and Jilmil were conspiring to shut down
the annual cultural programmes held on the occasions of
the Bihu and Durga Puja festivals. However, they had
another issue with him: His initiative of bringing back
the children working in the quarry.

In order to teach Anubhav a lesson, one day, these
young men brought some opportunistic TV journalists
to the village school. Their intention was to start a brawl
and get it on record to defame Anubhav and Jilmil.

Sloganeering and making aggressive gestures, they
started creating chaos in the school campus. Hearing the
commotion, the teachers rushed out. Terrified, the students

too left their classes to see what was going on. Standing on the veranda, everyone became a mute spectator to the drama that was unfolding in front of them.

'A teacher by the name of Anubhav here is embroiled in a scandal with a female teacher! We can't just sit and let this happen! We cannot turn a blind eye to this!' Just then, the other men gathered there started shouting, 'This can't go on! Can't go on! Dismiss Anubhav from the job! Dismiss him! Dismiss him!'

The TV crew got excited upon hearing such scandalous news, so they kept rolling the camera and recording the entire sequence of events.

Inside, the students were shocked. They couldn't understand what was going on. Why on earth would their beloved teacher be dismissed from service?

By now, Headmaster Sanatan was out of the veranda, requesting the youths to stop the sloganeering and to put forward their grievances calmly. However, the men were in no mood to see reason. They were more interested in creating an unruly, unsavoury scene. They knew that this was a great way to demoralize Anubhav and get him to leave the village.

After a while, the teachers' patience started wearing thin. This was unacceptable—to falsely accuse one of their own! Just then, a murmur started doing the rounds. Everyone noticed Mahendra sir coming out of the common room carrying not one or two but a big bundle of bamboo canes!

Sprinting towards the gate, brandishing a formidable cane, he went for the useless boys, who were suddenly dumbfounded! They didn't expect the teacher to come charging at them! Their sloganeering suddenly stopped.

Mahendra sir roared, 'Trying to be leaders, are you? This cane will tear your back apart, you fools! First, you yourself spoiled your own student life. Now that you have no alternative, are you trying to become useless leaders with frivolous agendas? You've come to destroy the school now, eh? Have you no better job? Ah, and look, you've brought a TV crew too! But did you even come to us before this? To talk about your issues? Have you even thought about the problems of the village ever, let alone the school?' he shouted. 'We've tolerated your nuisance for long. You don't care for the welfare of the school? No problem. But if you disrupt our sincere work, I'll break this cane on your backs. I'd given up using the cane for quite some time now. But you've made me pick it up again! Come, let me use it on you.'

On seeing Mahendra sir's energy and mood, the students cheered loudly! Pumped, they came running down, shouting. Within a few minutes, they surrounded the youth leaders from all sides, shutting off their escape routes!

Anubhav also came out of the veranda and went to the crowd. With his head held high, he walked directly towards the leaders. He'd realized by now that there was more to this than what was visible to the eye; a big conspiracy was afoot, and this was just a prelude.

'Tell me—what scandal you've seen me indulging in?' he asked them directly, unafraid, in front of the TV crew.

The committee men were taken aback by such a straightforward question. They hadn't thought that Anubhav would actually confront them! Fumbling and stuttering, one of them replied, 'The . . . the security guard knows what you did, okay!'

Hearing this, Jilmil who had also followed Anubhav along with the other teachers, burst into laughter. Sniggering and snorting, she then narrated to everyone that day's incident.

After listening to everything, Headmaster Sanatan gestured to the TV journalists. 'How is this drama "news" for you? Had Mahendra sir not brandished his cane, you would have broadcast this incident as breaking news! Aren't you ashamed of yourselves? A few days ago, a new library was inaugurated at our school. For the first time ever in the history of the village! Where were you folks then? The manner in which you have spoiled the atmosphere of our school today, I think I should lodge a complaint against you and these useless "youth leaders" at the local police station.'

The TV crew fumbled for a response. But the headmaster didn't stop for a reply, 'We are trying our best to improve the school and the lives of the village children. If you can, lend us a hand. If you can't, at least don't do things that will impede the future of the kids!'

64

Anubhav rushed to town. He'd received a phone call from Nirmal's father that the boy had been admitted to the hospital. At around 2 a.m., Nirmal had complained of chest pains, followed by intense sweating and breathing issues. So, without a moment's delay, an ambulance had been called. Nirmal's condition was so bad that for the entire journey, he was put on oxygen. Nirmal's father knew that in such a situation, every second counted and any sort of delay could be life threatening. Once they'd reached the hospital, Nirmal was immediately admitted to the intensive care unit (ICU).

Quite obviously, Anubhav was upset and worried. He loved Nirmal very much and felt for the boy and his parents. Their suffering was so massive that Anubhav had no words to console them. Every word seemed to fall short—harsh, insipid, incapable of conveying his feelings. He was in awe of the family too. Their resilience and strength was something else; he felt like saluting them!

Nirmal was still in the ICU when Anubhav reached the hospital. His parents were sitting, zombie-like, on a bench outside, with their heads resting against the wall. They stood up upon seeing Anubhav.

'How is Nirmal now?'

'Somewhat stable. He wanted to see you. That's why I rang you up,' said his father, softly.

Anubhav felt an intense urge to walk into the ICU and meet Nirmal right away. He wanted to gently pat Nirmal's forehead and tell him that everything would be all right. Anubhav's heart was awash with emotions. But he had to wait for two long hours before he could enter the ICU.

Somehow, the minutes dragged on.

Before entering, Anubhav meticulously observed the cleanliness protocols of the ICU. Thereafter, opening the door, Anubhav entered the room. Nirmal was lying motionless on the bed, his eyes shut, and an oxygen mask covered his mouth and nose. ECG wires were attached to his chest and legs. The boy was still except for the heavy breaths that he was taking. The surgery gash on his chest was quite clearly visible.

As Anubhav entered the room, an unfamiliar and strong odour of a concoction of medicines hit him at once. The quietness of the ICU hall was disturbed by the intermittent 'beeping' from the various medical instruments. Treading carefully, he reached Nirmal's bed. Glancing at the readings on the monitor, Anubhav could infer that Nirmal was not out of danger yet. He felt terrible. The boy with such a beautiful heart was in so much unnecessary pain. It was unbearable to see him lying like this on the ICU bed. Anubhav felt like touching Nirmal's forehead gently with affection. *But what if he woke up? Best to let him rest.*

Anubhav was given only three minutes to see his dear student. After a minute of watching him sleep, he broke his restraint and put his hand on the boy's forehead. Nirmal opened his eyes slowly. It took a few seconds for Nirmal to recognize who it was. As he did, he instantly tried to sit up. But Anubhav shook his head and, holding Nirmal by the hand, gently laid him back on the bed again.

Nirmal kept looking at Anubhav with a fixed glance. To escape that benign glance, which was piercing Anubhav's heart, he asked him, 'How are you feeling?'

Nirmal didn't answer. He kept looking at his teacher's face till his eyes welled up with tears.

'The world,' he whispered through the oxygen mask. 'The world is such a beautiful place, sir. You . . . you are there, Ashim is there and my . . . my parents are there. You know, sir . . . recently, I planted a bakul tree in my yard. I think, over time, it will grow into a big tree with lots of branches and leaves.' He paused to rest. 'And soon, glorious bakul flowers will sprout. I wish . . . I . . . I yearn to live long enough to see them flower, sir,' saying this, Nirmal started panting out of exhaustion.

. 'I want to live for long . . . I yearn to live long . . . sir!'

It was as if something very heavy was thrust upon Anubhav's chest. He breathed hard and choked with tears. 'You will . . . you will live long enough, Nirmal, long enough!'

At that moment, Nirmal's earnest wish combined with the hopes of Anubhav, turned into an earnest prayer. It travelled like the fragrance of incense burning in the sanctum sanctorum of the village temple. But where was this temple? For Anubhav, who recognized himself as an agnostic—to whom should his prayer be directed?

Anubhav felt very helpless. He earnestly wished Nirmal and all the other patients in the ICU would heal fast. He hoped the hospital room—which was now filled with the strong odour of various chemicals and medicines and the beeping noise of instruments— would turn into a temple filled with the fragrance of sweet-smelling incense and the pleasant ring of the temple bell and pure sound of conch shell would reverberate here! *Let the doctors be actual gods and grant a long life to the residents of the ICU!* With that intense hope in his heart, Anubhav exited the ICU.

As he walked out with his head bowed, he saw that someone else was waiting. Sitting on the floor outside the ICU, sobbing uncontrollably, was Ashim.

65

'Earlier, I used to think there is enough time to give all the good things in the world to Nirmal, to give something back to the people, too. And suddenly, one day, I realized, no! There isn't much time. There is no certainty in this life, Anubhav. Life can deceive us at any moment. Whatever I can give Nirmal, whatever I can give the others, I have to do it today. I have to give back at this very moment. The good things which need to be done ought to be done as early as possible.'

It seemed like Nirmal's father had aged overnight. 'He's my heart and soul. I feel like wrapping Nirmal with all the warmth of the heart . . . I feel like introducing him to all the beautiful things of this world that he hasn't yet seen, today itself! I feel like replacing all the pain and agony that life has dealt him with all the happiness of this world . . .' Nirmal's father had opened up to Anubhav before his visit to the ICU. He was too heavy with grief.

Now, waiting in front of the ICU again, this time alone, Anubhav thought about the words of a father in pain. His mind felt very heavy. To divert his mind, Anubhav opened the newspaper that someone had left behind on the bench.

'Embezzlement of lakhs of rupees by high-ranking official . . .' the headline read.

Anubhav's heart sank. Disgusted, he crumpled the newspaper and threw it into the litter bin outside the ICU.

66

For some days now, a sort of suspicion regarding Ashim's father had taken hold of Anubhav's mind.

Of late, there prevailed some kind of orderliness at their house. But Anubhav was restless, thinking about other possibilities: *Would Ashim's father create a ruckus again? I don't like the man hawking the newspapers upon which Ashim's livelihood depends.* Anubhav wondered if the man wanted to take over the newspaper agency. Was he thinking of taking all the money for himself and spending it on liquor again? If that were to happen, it would not only create a problem for the whole family but for the agency as well, which Anubhav had set up with a lot of hard work. Moreover, not much time was left for Ashim's board exams. And at a time like this, no such untoward event could be allowed to happen, Anubhav decided. *Yes, I must talk directly to him,* he resolved.

Anubhav waited outside his veranda on this present morning. Just when Ashim's father came to deliver the newspaper, he stopped the man.

'I want to talk to you about something.'

'Tell me.'

'Why have you started distributing the newspapers?' Anubhav asked bluntly.

'What? Why are you asking me this?'

'Just tell me.'

'Actually, I want Ashim to study properly . . . his exams are coming up.'

'That's very good,' Anubhav said, pausing, 'but who will keep the money from the agency?'

Hearing this harsh question, the man looked a bit hurt. He kept gazing at Anubhav helplessly. But Anubhav didn't turn away his face; he demanded answers.

'Tell me,' he asked again, 'who would get to keep the money? You or Ashim?'

'Ashim,' the man said quietly.

'If you are doing the job allured by the money or with the hope of taking over the agency over time, then you should stop right away,' said Anubhav, without mincing his words.

The man stayed quiet. After a while, he said, 'Okay, on the last two days of every month, Ashim will distribute the newspapers and collect the money.'

Am I being too harsh on the man, more than what is necessary? thought Anubhav. *No, no*, he reasoned. He had come to care for the boy like his own son, and he had seen the mental trauma he had undergone. Anubhav couldn't let that happen to Ashim again. Anyway, these months were very crucial for Ashim. If anything untoward were to happen now, everything he'd worked so hard for would come to naught. *It takes very little for things to get spoiled, but it takes far more time to bring those things back into working order again.*

*

Anubhav noticed the man was still standing there. He had nothing left to say to him. So, Anubhav asked him, 'Do you have anything that you want to say to me?'

'No.' The man shook his head. 'I was just listening to the song. Feels good.'

It was only then that Anubhav noticed the melodious song coming from inside his room.

> The autumnal night jasmines paint the ground
>> And dew drops gather on blades of grass
> In the moonlight, something intoxicates the air
>> And the mind begins to feel so restless
>
> Oh! My dear friend
>> The mind indeed starts to feel restless.
>
> Donning a turban of snowy white clouds
>> Which Prince Charming arrives
> At the crack of dawn, on my doorstep,
>> And into my house he peeps?
>
> Oh! My dear friend
>> The mind indeed starts to feel restless.

The companion of my soul,
        Have I met you before once?
Along the lane with fallen night jasmine blooms
        I feel I've seen you at one glance.

I won't linger to enumerate if I know you or not
        As an unknown adoration washes over me
The crazy recluse that lives inside my heart
        Today, a joyful dance of love sets him free!

Oh! My dear friend
        The mind indeed starts to feel restless.

'Such a beautiful song! Feels as if I'm listening to a prayer,' the man said spiritedly, closing his eyes.

Anubhav was taken aback. It is said that when Parvati Prasad Barua, the lyricist of this beautiful song, sang this song to his mother for the very first time, she too told him the very same thing that Ashim's father had just shared with Anubhav.

'Though it's not autumn now, dew drops are falling relentlessly. Such a soothing experience, isn't it, Anubhav sir? Listening to this song in this atmosphere. Ah!'

Anubhav realized the man too was overwhelmed by the lyrics. The man prepared to leave and remarked, 'We don't have any provision for listening to such songs, nor do we have the time.' He sighed.

'What?' Anubhav asked, confused.

'I meant, where will I get money to purchase that expensive machine on which to listen to these songs?

And where is the time for people like us to listen to such songs anyway? We don't get to sit around in the comfort of our homes. We have to toil every waking hour, don't we? The only time we do get to listen to them is when the stores at the market square play them.'

67

Anubhav was shell-shocked by Ashim's father's profound utterance!

Anubhav's thoughts on the topic echoed the sentiments of many intellectuals who lamented the general shallowness in people's taste, be it in literature, music and other cultural aspects of our society now. Serious literature, songs and movies are not typically popular. Mediocre creations often outshine superior ones in terms of popularity. This is, in fact, a crisis. He wondered, *Are the paucity of opportunities and privileges, and the relentless struggle for survival really responsible for this crisis?* Anubhav recalled a debate between two highbrow intellectuals who had decried that high culture and meaningful artistic pursuits were reserved for the affluent and the privileged classes. Anubhav couldn't agree more with their criticism. *How can financial hardships be the sole catalyst behind this crisis? I have seen with my own eyes how Ashim's father, despite his penury, always manages to scrape together money for his daily dose of alcohol,* he thought.

But then, Anubhav also witnessed it himself: how this man left Anubhav's place only after the song finished playing. It implied if meaningful music had a natural place in our society, it would have certainly reached the masses. Anubhav believed that intellectual apathy bore more responsibility for this crisis than money or the lack thereof.

The popularity of inane television soaps in our households could be attributed to the intellectual indolence of the masses. Anubhav reasoned that the masses are satisfied with superficial things and do not want to engage with profound issues. *The pervasive negative impact of religion on our society cannot be attributed to economic backwardness alone, as some often believe,* he thought. Here also, people's intellectual apathy is more to blame.

Anubhav believed that real and meaningful change had to start within the education system. A generation free from intellectual lethargy could only stem from sincere efforts. Schools and colleges should include intellectual exercises and not just physical ones. Literary creations, scientific models, debates and discussions should not just be the stuff of competitions and exhibitions held annually but must be an integral part of students' lives. It should be ingrained in their psyche that those sorts of intellectual exercises are part of their normal existence. Intellectual rigour should become second nature to students and only then could these citizens of tomorrow be expected to build a better society conducive to serious art forms.

It was not as if Anubhav was just stuck in despair. He had, with the help of his colleagues, begun this change.

They had established a library in their school, stocking it with a curated collection of books and the opportunity to appreciate good music. He knew that the importance of the education system could not be confined to conventional notions anymore or the damage to society would become irreversible. Education must be thought of deeply by all stakeholders. Despite his insights and action, Anubhav still felt powerless. He wondered to whom he could confide these thoughts swirling like a whirlpool in his mind. The feeling of helplessness threatened to plunge his sanity into the depths of this whirlpool of worry. After all, he was just an ordinary schoolteacher; what could he do?

But 'hope is the thing with feathers', so a glimmer of hope emerged as Anubhav considered his school and the positive atmosphere he had striven to create through his convictions. His colleagues and students also supported him wholeheartedly. This gave him some comfort.

68

Since Nirmal's return from the hospital, Ashim spent most of his time with his best friend. As Nirmal was still very weak, he couldn't study on his own for the boards. So, for the last few days, Ashim had been assisting him.

As Nirmal lay on his bed, Ashim would sit beside him and read the chapters aloud. And Nirmal would listen and revise in his mind.

One day, Ashim noticed that Nirmal was not paying attention. Lying on the bed, he was gazing out of the window, absentmindedly.

'What happened?' he asked Nirmal.

'What do you mean?'

'Why aren't you listening to what I am reading?' Ashim asked.

'No! I'm listening.'

'C'mon! Don't lie!'

Ashim noticed that Nirmal had turned sombre. He didn't say anything and continued to look out of the window.

'What's wrong?'

'You are wasting your time on me every day, Ashim. Won't it affect your studies?' Nirmal sighed.

'Don't I study by your side daily?' Ashim replied angrily.

'Still . . .' said Nirmal. 'When one studies by themselves, one can retain more information and study more effectively.'

'So when you tried to bring me back to school and sat with me, your studies suffered too?'

'Oh, so you are repaying the debt?' Nirmal queried, with a weak smile.

'Are you kidding me?' Ashim said, annoyed. 'Can anyone even repay such debts?'

'Forget it,' Nirmal said, shrugging. 'Let's go to the foothill!'

Ashim was shocked. He knew that Nirmal was very weak physically after his stint at the hospital. 'Are you mad? Why to the foothill?' shouted Ashim in fright.

'To look for Ramen and his mates,' said Nirmal, sitting up.

In his heart of hearts, Ashim knew why Nirmal wanted to do this. But still he asked. 'Why?'

'They too have to come to school again, don't they?'

Ashim recalled the time when Nirmal had come searching for him and Ramen had taunted him. It had enraged Ashim so much that he had wanted to beat up Ramen!

'No need for you and me to worry about those things right now,' Ashim said. 'Our teachers have already visited their homes and have started talks with their family members.'

'No. Let's go and meet them, Ashim. Ramen and the others will feel good,' saying this, Nirmal got down from the bed, and holding Ashim's hand, he walked outside.

69

The board exams were finally over. Everyone had been expecting a stellar performance from Nirmal. But as he'd fallen sick at the last moment, that expectation had more or less diminished. Nirmal's parents had also not put him under any such pressure; they just wanted their child to get well.

The teachers were hopeful for Ashim too, who had made rapid progress in the last few months leading up to the exams. However, due to the chaos in his life, nobody was expecting a phenomenal performance from him as well.

Although nobody said anything to anyone openly, everyone was a bit demoralized. Even Anubhav was a bit dejected thanks to the recent events.

*

The day after the exams were over, the two boys met at Nirmal's house. They brought out all the question papers and had long discussions about the possible answers. Both Nirmal and Ashim were happy; they felt that they had done fairly well in the exams.

But they just couldn't decide who had fared better—Ashim or Nirmal?

70

Finally, the day when the results would be declared arrived.

Anxious students, along with their equally nervous parents, crowded the school campus long before the results were out. Everybody waited impatiently outside the teachers' common room. And inside, the teachers sat with similar levels of anxiety as the parents.

Away from all others, near the school gate, Ashim was sitting under his leafy bakul tree—the same tree that had been planted by his father many years ago. In that tree, Ashim had always sought a sense of security, something which his own father had failed to provide.

Sitting there under the tree's shade, last year's incident kept playing out in his mind in a loop. That day too, he had been waiting for his results. All alone. Before Mahendra sir had slapped him and said, 'You're ruined'.

Ashim remembered everything vividly. He looked at the thumb of his left hand. The scar was still there.

Perhaps, it would be there forever as a reminder of his past self.

Just like in the movies, flashbacks of old memories kept playing out in his mind in quick succession. He had no high ambition regarding his performance in this exam. Even the teachers were not expecting any miracles from him. His poor parents didn't even have a clue as to what constituted good or bad results. Thanks to all of this, he didn't feel too anxious. His only concern was to please Nirmal and Anubhav sir. If he managed to perform well, both would be extremely happy, and all his struggles would be worth it.

'Will you keep sitting here? Do you have any intention of coming inside?' Nirmal asked Ashim. He had crept up on his friend, who had been lost in his own thoughts.

'Actually, I should not have been sitting here at all. It is because of you and Anubhav sir that I'm here,' Ashim said, feeling a little emotional.

Nirmal nodded. He understood that Ashim was thinking about old incidents and also trying to avoid Mahendra sir, even after all this time.

'Oh, right. Because of us you've been able to sit under the bakul tree only, all alone! So sorry!' said Nirmal with a smile.

'Don't say it like that. I'll get the results here as well. You go inside!'

'Nah . . . let's just sit here.' Nirmal smiled.

*

At 11 a.m. sharp, Headmaster Sanatan opened the packet containing the results. He searched for the page according to the centre number. Both Ashim and Nirmal had secured first division! There was a star mark against each of the two roll numbers. It meant both had managed to secure 'star marks', that is, distinctions that Assam's school board, the Secondary Education Board of Assam or SEBA, had designated. Four other students had secured first-division marks. The teachers were elated! After scanning the list, they declared: All the students except one had passed. Before this year, no one would have thought that they would witness such a day! Previously, the matriculation results had never been this glorious. It was an unimaginable feat for the students and the school! The atmosphere in the school immediately became festive.

Jilmil took the result booklet from the headmaster. Perusing and counting the subjects with 'letter marks', that is, subjects in which the marks were above 80 per cent according to SEBA, Jilmil found that both Nirmal and Ashim had received letter marks in all subjects. Jubilant, she turned the pages and opened the first page. Everybody noticed Jilmil's eyes pop, her hands shiver and her lips tremble. And after a few seconds, she burst out aloud with unbridled joy, 'Both Nirmal and Ashim have secured ranks on an all-Assam level. Nirmal has come third in the state, and Ashim has managed to get the seventh rank!'

A wave of jubilation spread across the school and emanated in all directions. Everyone shouted in joy, hugging each other and dancing. Jilmil jumped up and down like a little girl!

'But where are those two idiots?' roared Mahendra master.

*

Ashim and Nirmal could hear a commotion from the school. It seemed there was a huge uproar from the direction of the teachers' common room. Ashim and Nirmal looked at each other nervously. Before they could figure out what was happening, they saw a man rush towards them as if chased by a supernatural entity. Following him was a group of people dancing and jumping along!

'Mahendra sir?' mumbled the two.

Mahendra sir halted under the bakul tree. The procession following him, too, froze there. Someone, unable to hold it in, shouted out their results. Both the boys were shell-shocked. Before they could get a word in edgewise, Mahendra sir shouted, 'Why are you two hiding away?' Saying this, he jumped forward and hugged Nirmal tightly.

Frightened, Ashim took three steps backwards.

There was a big pen in Mahendra sir's pocket that was digging into Nirmal's skin when Mahendra master hugged him tightly. He felt as if his teacher wouldn't set him free!

At last, leaving Nirmal alone, Mahendra master looked for Ashim.

'And where are you fleeing to, you idiot?'

Mahendra master grabbed Ashim and pulled him into a warm embrace.

Is my teacher crying? Ashim wondered as he felt the body of Mahendra sir shaking intermittently.

'Didn't I tell you—you are the jewel of our school, Ashim,' said Mahendra sir.

Everyone was shocked to see Mahendra sir openly sobbing while hugging Ashim.

71

Anubhav noticed the same TV crew who had come to the school the other day, waiting stealthily outside the school gate. Anubhav felt bad for them. He went to them and invited them inside.

'Perhaps you've realized today that no scandal was going on in our school. But a different kind of news was in the making!'

The crew looked down in shame.

'Securing a rank in the board exams is not a very big issue,' said Anubhav to the crew. 'What's important is the story of the boys' struggles and how they overcame them,' he said proudly. 'Do you know, while one of these kids has been struggling against the hostile environment at his own home, the other one has been fighting a congenital disease? What is even more important is that, unlike other brilliant students, they are not selfish or egotistical. Not only are they strong-willed but they are sensitive human beings also.'

Brimming with pride, Anubhav went on speaking spiritedly about Nirmal and Ashim. 'You know, the majority of our journalists look for only negative news nowadays. Whatever positive news they publish or broadcast, they don't know how to present it in a wholesome manner,' he said. 'So, if you do go ahead, please publish the news about Nirmal and Ashim in such a way that people feel encouraged after hearing their story. Ensure that your viewers get to see their fight against the odds against their sufferings. While presenting today's news, please don't use Nirmal's congenital disease or the hostile environment surrounding Ashim's life as tools for increasing the television rating points (TRPs) of your channel. Please don't crush their beautiful minds ruthlessly in your mad rush to climb the TRPs.'

Anubhav now noticed the so-called student leaders had arrived as well. They were lurking behind some parents.

Seeing the camera crew, they started speaking loudly, 'We always had faith in our locals! As you can see, we have nothing to worry about now. The likes of Ashim and Nirmal will develop our village.' Saying this, they started shouting, 'Nirmal-Ashim Zindabad!'

Irritated by this façade, Jilmil jumped into the fray, 'Excuse me, Zindabad Dada. Nirmal and Ashim have not won any election that you people are shouting zindabad. And what did you just say? Nirmal and Ashim will solve all the problems of our village? Wow, let's clap!' she said sarcastically. 'Since you adults have entrusted these underage teenagers with such a huge responsibly, all the

4000 residents of this village can sleep peacefully now and can afford to twiddle their thumbs!'

Just then, a few stray cattle strolled into the campus and relieved themselves on the school grounds. Seeing this Mahendra sir came out with a long cane to drive them away. The so-called leaders remembering last time's incident, got scared! They recalled how the man had run towards them with the cane! 'Let's go . . . we have . . . um . . . work . . . getting late,' muttering so, they ran away.

The TV crew started laughing. 'Don't worry, sir. We won't broadcast any of their bytes. We kept the camera rolling just to satisfy these fools,' said one journalist with a smile.

Mahendra walked upto Anubhav. Looking towards the camera crew, he shifted uneasily. 'Leave these TVs and cameras, Anubhav. Let the boys remain the way they are.'

72

Sitting on the muddy veranda of her house, Ashim's mother was eagerly looking towards the road. She was unsettled and nervous. Suddenly, Ajoli darted through the gate like a bull and stopped as she reached her mother. 'What happened, Ajoli?'

Out of breath due to excitement, Ajoli panted and breathed hard. 'Dada . . . Dada . . . and Nirmal dada too . . .'

Ajoli stopped to catch her breath. Her mother, already extremely anxious, was now more restless seeing her daughter in such a state! 'What? What? Tell me!' she shrieked.

'Both . . . both of them secured ranks in the boards, Ma!' Ajoli cried.

Ashim's mother sat there, speechless and stupefied. She kept looking at Ajoli with eyes as big as saucers. Gradually, her eyes welled up with tears under the unbearable weight of her emotions. She felt happiness, sorrow and gratitude all at once.

Do people cry even when they hear such happy news? Ajoli never understood this type of reaction to good news! Nor did she have any patience for it! And so the little girl darted out through the gate again. After all, she had to give the happy news to so many of her friends!

73

A shim's father got the news in the liquor shop.
Hearing this, the man was dumbfounded for a while. Thereafter, in a proud posture of declaring something, he started to speak: 'In this happy hour of Ashim's result . . .' saying this, the man raised a bottle in the air. His companions clapped in anticipation of a huge feast with meat and alcohol at night, sponsored by Ashim's father.

Just then, the man brought down the bottle with force and completed his declaration: 'Hereby, I give up drinking alcohol for good.'

Falling to the ground, the glass bottle shattered into a hundred pieces.

Ashim's father now darted from the liquor shop in search of his son.

74

Crystal-clear moonlight bathed everything outside. Anubhav opened the window. A beam of moonlight passed through the window and lay scattered on his bed. A gust of a soothing cold breeze followed. The brushing of the coconut fronds made a rustling sound that travelled to his ears. The day had passed in festive spirit, and now the atmosphere of the village appeared quieter. Anubhav saw a few stray dogs running here and there. Except for a couple of vegetable vendors returning from far-off villages after the day's business, the road in front of his house was almost deserted.

Anubhav sat on the chair by the side of his window. On such beautiful moonlit nights, he felt a restlessness within. Old memories of his cheerful bygone days would invariably come rushing to him, tearing his heart apart. And no, those can't be shared with anyone. Some memories are very personal. And they disappear only with one's death.

A beautiful melody from a flute could be heard now wafting towards him from a distance. Anubhav listened intently. *Perhaps someone was playing the flute in despair. There is pathos in the tune of a flute,* he thought, sighing.

This poignant melody especially on this quiet night stabbed Anubhav's heart like a knife would.

Who is playing this flute? Should I go outside and search for the source of this melancholy music?

Suddenly, the harsh ring of his cell phone startled him. He picked up the call.

'Hey Anubhav. Can't you see how lovely the moonlight is today?'

Anubhav was taken aback. Never had Jilmil spoken to him so casually.

'Oh, c'mon! Open the window and look outside . . . the moonlight is everywhere. You know what, I feel like singing! Will you listen if I sing?'

Jilmil had never been a girl who would wait for anyone to grant her permission. Pouring out all her emotions, she sang:

In the woods, there was no moonlight
In the mind, there was no moonlight
Star to star, the conversation flowed
To the deepest core of the heart.

The twilight's gentle breeze
Ebbed and flowed in waves
Upon the gilded sky!

In the woods, there was no moonlight
In the mind, there was no moonlight
Clusters of stars were weaving a tune
Creating a harmony for your new song!

Anubhav was pleasantly surprised—*Ah, that old song!*
It reverberated in the deepest recesses of his heart even
today. Snigdha had sung it to him so many times. Every
full moon night had brought this song to him like a gust
of a soft breeze.

Has Snigdha come back? Or is she sinking into oblivion forever?

'You know, Anubhav, unlike the song, today there is
moonlight even in the woods . . . and, if I can be honest,
there is moonlight in my mind too. Hello? Hello? Hey
Anubhav, why aren't you saying anything? Please say
something . . . for my sake, please?' Jilmil's pleas gradually
got lost in the bleak emptiness of the night.

Anubhav became more restless than before. Memories
that he had pushed down and repressed were impatiently
threatening to emerge to the surface. His eyes were
tearing up.

The melancholic tone of the flute broke through the
night again.

Anubhav came out to the veranda. His legs
automatically took him to the road. Following the
melody of the flute, Anubhav arrived at the gate of his
student Simanta's compound.

Sitting on the bamboo platform under the bakul tree
at their gate, the boy was playing the flute, pouring out
all his emotions into it.

Oh!

Simanta was the boy who failed the exam today. Except for him, all the others had passed.

Seeing Anubhav, Simanta lowered his head. The otherwise jubilant boy had become pale and lifeless today.

A few abuses being hurled at Simanta came to Anubhav's ears. 'He is the black sheep of our family! All my prestige is lost. How will he pass if he loiters around day in and day out with that idiotic flute in his hand?'

Simanta's father seemed to be angry and was rebuking the boy loudly.

Tears rolled down Simanta's cheeks. He clutched at his flute.

'Feeling very sad, Simanta?'

'Everyone . . . everyone passed except me.' Waiting a while, he uttered faintly, 'It is only I who—'

'It is only you who can play the flute so very beautifully,' Anubhav completed the sentence. 'No one else in our school can play the flute this melodiously.'

Anubhav noticed that suddenly Simanta started to get twitchy, his lips trembled, and his eyes became moist. Soon, the boy broke down.

75

In the chaos of the day, Ashim and Nirmal didn't get the opportunity to talk to each other. Even though Ashim had been in Nirmal's house since evening, they didn't get a quiet minute to themselves. People were flocking to the house to meet both of them. It was only after 10 p.m. that the number of visitors gradually dwindled and finally everyone left. After which, Nirmal's parents requested Ashim to have dinner with them before leaving for home.

Nirmal and Ashim were finally alone. Both of them walked towards the compound's gate.

Bright moonlight flooded the road in front of the house.

A few months back, Nirmal had planted a bakul sapling in the front yard. Ashim could see in the moonlight that the sprig had grown steadily. Silently, both of them observed the plant.

They didn't know what had come over them today. Earlier, they used to talk so much, and today, they had no words to say to each other.

Finally, Nirmal turned to look at his best friend. So did Ashim.

Nirmal noticed that Ashim's lips had started to tremble and that he was blinking rapidly, fighting off tears. Both remained quiet. At one point, Nirmal noticed that Ashim's eyes were finally filled with unshed tears. Unlike other days, Ashim didn't turn away his face. Today, he didn't try to hide his feelings.

Surprised, Nirmal asked, 'You are crying, Ashim?'

'So are you, Nirmal!' replied his best friend.

Acknowledgements

Heartfelt gratitude to Devabrata Das, Dr Meenaxi Barkataki, Kusum Kalita, Mamata Devi Goswami and Anup Kumar Das for their encouragement.

Dr Madan Mohan Sarma for constant guidance and support.

Arpita Nath for commissioning the book.

Yasmin Rahman for refining the translation.

And Sushmita Chatterjee and the entire PRH team for making the book impeccable.

The Room on the Roof

Ruskin Bond

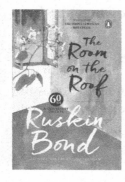

A classic coming-of-age story which has held generations of readers spellbound!

Rusty, a sixteen-year-old Anglo-Indian boy, is orphaned and has to live with his English guardian in the claustrophobic European part in Dehra Dun. Unhappy with the strict ways of his guardian, Rusty runs away from home to live with his Indian friends. Plunging for the first time into the dream-bright world of the bazaar, Hindu festivals and other aspects of Indian life, Rusty is enchanted . . . and is lost forever to the prim proprieties of the European community.

Written when the author was himself seventeen, this moving story of love and friendship, with a new introduction and illustrations will be enjoyed by a whole new generation of readers.

READ MORE IN PUFFIN

Puffin Classics: Vagrants in the Valley
Ruskin Bond

An evergreen classic about friendship and growing up, by a master storyteller.

This book catches us up with our favourite Rusty as he plunges not just into the cold pools of Dehra but into an exciting new life, dipping his toes into adulthood.

Winding his way back to the city with Kishen, Rusty discovers that his beloved room is no longer his! Undaunted, and in his trademark style, he forges new homes and new friendships as he embarks on a journey of self-discovery that spans the beautiful hillsides of India.

By turns thrilling and nostalgic, this heart-warming sequel finds Rusty at his best as he navigates the tightrope between dreams and reality, all the time maintaining a glorious sense of hope. Striking, evocative, witty and wise—this is an ode to youth and all its complexities, amidst the colours, sights and smells of Bond's India.

READ MORE IN PUFFIN

Puffin Classics: Shyamchi Aai
Sane Guruji (Tr. Shanta Gokhale)

A Marathi classic on the unbreakable spirit of a mother's love.

The evening prayers in the ashram are over. Cowbells tinkle sweetly in the distance. The residents of the ashram sit in a circle, their eyes fixed on Shyam, who has promised them a story as sweet as lemon syrup. And so Shyam begins.

While on some evenings he tells them of his boyhood days, surrounded by the abundant beauty of the Konkan, on others he recalls growing up poor, embarrassed by the state of his family's affairs. But at the heart of each story is his Aai-her words and lessons. He reminisces of the day his mother showed him the importance of honesty and the time she went hungry just so her children could eat a full meal.

Narrated over the course of forty-two nights, *Shyamchi Aai* is a poignant story of Shyam and Aai, a mother with an unbreakable spirit. This evergreen classic, now translated by the incomparable Shanta Gokhale, is an account of a life of poverty, hard work, sacrifice and love.

Scan QR code to access the
Penguin Random House India website